For my grandparents: for the blood, for the wisdom, for the tender wounds we inherited with your love. Your ghosts are in my dreams.
~ Marjorie

It is everywhere, but fewer people perceive it. I keep seeing it.
~ Sana

MONSTRESS™

VOLUME TWO
THE BLOOD

Collecting
MONSTRESS
Issues 7 - 12

MARJORIE LIU
WRITER

SANA TAKEDA
ARTIST

RUS WOOTON
LETTERING & DESIGN

JENNIFER M. SMITH
EDITOR

CERI RILEY
EDITORIAL ASSISTANT

MONSTRESS
created by
MARJORIE LIU &
SANA TAKEDA

GN MONSTRESS V.2

CHAPTER SEVEN

"MISS? I WOKE UP LAST NIGHT, AND YOU WERE GONE."
"I WENT FOR A WALK, LITTLE FOX.
"I WAS... RESTLESS."

"OH.
"IT'S JUST... I HEARD PEOPLE TALKING BENEATH THE WINDOW THIS MORNING.
"THEY SAID... A MONSTER HAD SLAUGHTERED SHEEP DOWN BY THE DOCKS.
"I WONDERED...
"...IF YOU'D GOTTEN... *HUNGRY.*"
"YOU WANT TO KNOW IF THE MONSTER IS AWAKE."

THYRIA, MOST BELOVED CITY OF THE WAVE EMPRESS.
"YES, MISS. I HAVEN'T SEEN IT SINCE THE BATTLE WITH THE WITCHES."
"THAT'S BECAUSE IT'S SLEEPING AGAIN."
MOTHERFUCKER.
ARE YOU REALLY ASLEEP?
IF YOU CAN HEAR ME...YOUR DAYS ARE NUMBERED. I'M GOING TO TEAR YOU OUT OF ME IF IT'S THE LAST THING I DO.
I SWEAR AN OATH ON IT.

"The world breaks us all," you once said to me.
"But strength can flow from those broken places.
"Made new, in ways we never dreamed."
I'm trying to remember that, mother. I'm trying to remember you.
DOES IT HURT, MISS?
YES.
NOW STEP BACK. I NEED TO DRESS.
I can still feel you.
YOUR MOTHER HAD SUCH BEAUTIFUL THINGS.
...BUT MISS? YOU TOLD LORD CORVIN THAT YOU WERE POOR.
I SAID I GREW UP IN THE DIRT. AND I DID.
FOR MY MOTHER THIS WASN'T A HOME. IT WAS A BASE. I BARELY REMEMBER LIVING HERE BEFORE WE LEFT FOR THE DESERT.

...you're in this room filled with your obsession... the Shaman-Empress.

WE'RE MISSING SOMETHING. THE LAST TIME I WAS HERE IT WAS JUST A SUSPICION, BUT NOW I CAN FEEL IT IN MY BONES. THERE'S SOMETHING IMPORTANT WE HAVEN'T FOUND.

BUT WE'VE SEARCHED EVERYWHERE, MISS.

FUCK IT. I DON'T HAVE TIME FOR THIS.

CRACK

PING

DON'T TOUCH IT, MISS. THERE'S DEATH ON THAT KEY.

GOOD.

WELL, HELLO. YOU'RE FROM THE NORTH, AREN'T YOU, LITTLE ONE?

YES, MA'AM. HOW DID YOU KNOW?

NOT MANY FOXES IN THIS CITY. MOST OF THEM ARE REFUGEES.

DON'T WORRY...
THOSE SOLDIERS WON'T HURT YOU. THERE'S NO SLAVE TRADE HERE.
THE QUEENS OF THYRIA WOULD NEVER ALLOW SUCH MADNESS.

AND WHILE THOSE QUEENS HOLD THE ABYSSAL SEA, NEITHER THE FEDERATION OF MAN NOR THE CUMAEA WOULD DARE--
DON'T FEED THE CHILD LIES.
THYRIA WAS BRUTALLY INVADED ONCE ALREADY BY THE WITCHES. IT CAN HAPPEN AGAIN.

THE WAVE EMPRESS HERSELF SAVED THYRIA DURING THE WAR.
THE CUMAEA WILL NEVER FORGET THAT. THEY NOW FEAR THE GODDESS OF THE DEEP MORE THAN THEY REVERE THEIR FALSE MARIUM.
YOU KNOW NADA, OLD WOMAN. THE CUMAEA LOVE POWER MORE THAN THEY CARE ABOUT ANY GODDESS -- THEIR OWN, OR ANOTHER.
YOU SHOULD ALWAYS *MMPH* BE CAREFUL WITH WITCHES.

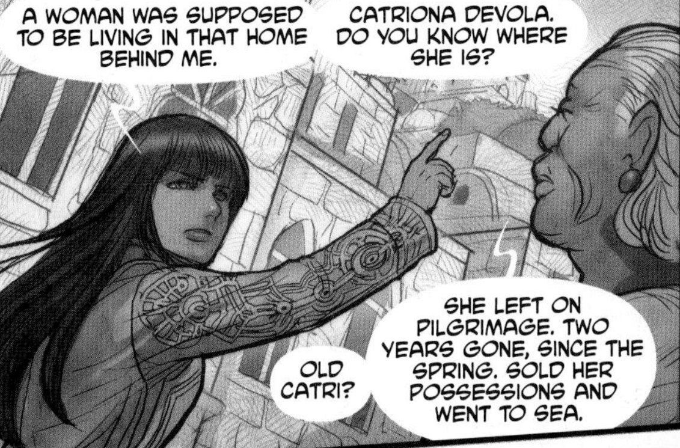
A WOMAN WAS SUPPOSED TO BE LIVING IN THAT HOME BEHIND ME.
CATRIONA DEVOLA. DO YOU KNOW WHERE SHE IS?
OLD CATRI?
SHE LEFT ON PILGRIMAGE. TWO YEARS GONE, SINCE THE SPRING. SOLD HER POSSESSIONS AND WENT TO SEA.

LET'S GO.
MISS? ARE WE GOING TO LOOK FOR THAT WOMAN WHO WENT AWAY?
NOT YET, LITTLE FOX. I HAVE SOMETHING ELSE TO TAKE CARE OF FIRST.

IS IT HER?
YES, YOUR MAJESTY. MORIKO HALFWOLF'S DAUGHTER HAS RETURNED.

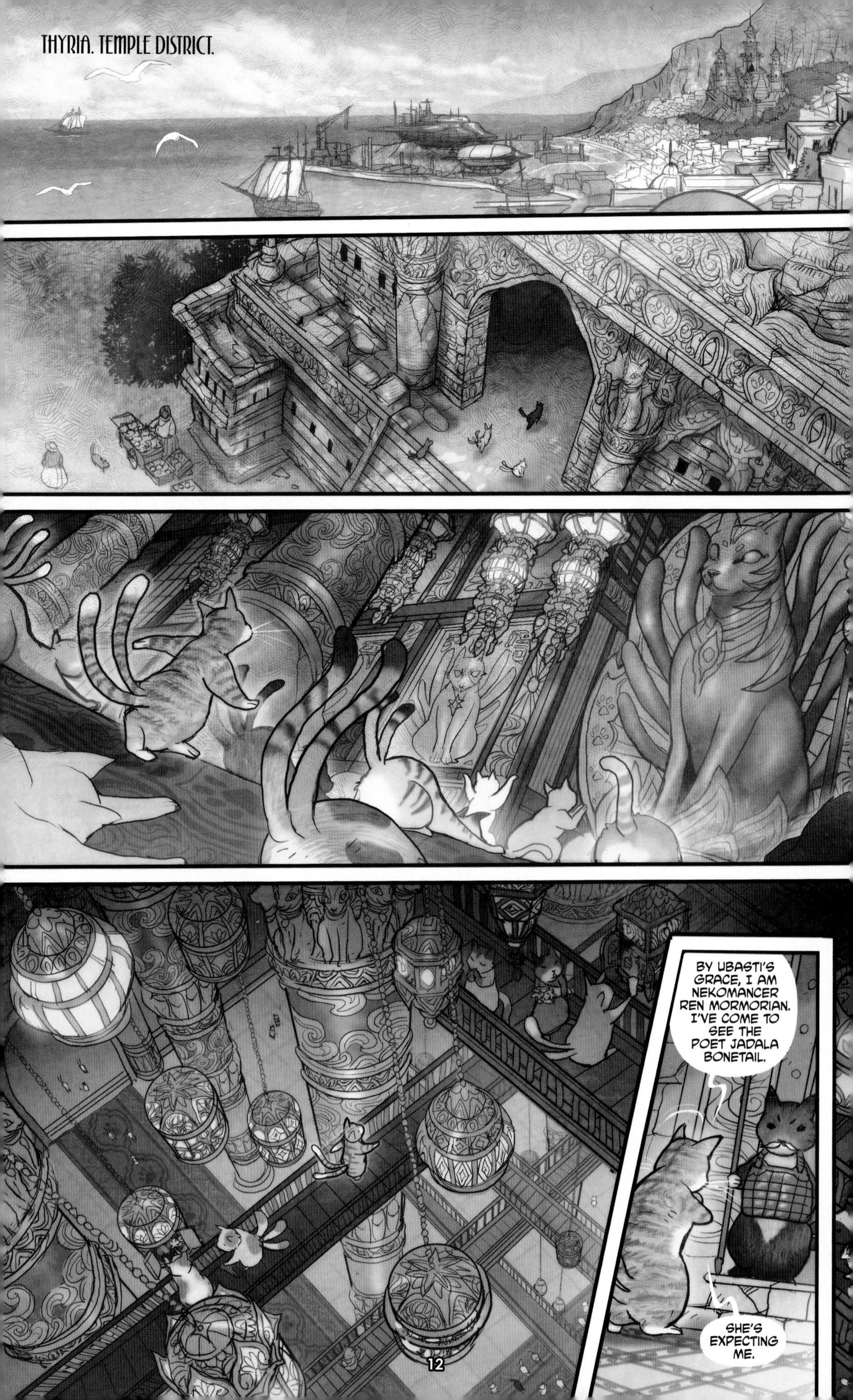

THYRIA. TEMPLE DISTRICT.

BY UBASTI'S GRACE, I AM NEKOMANCER REN MORMORIAN. I'VE COME TO SEE THE POET JADALA BONETAIL.

SHE'S EXPECTING ME.

DO YOU KNOW WHAT THE FIRST POET SAID ABOUT OUR KIND, YOUNG REN?
CATS ARE THE GREAT MYSTERY, BORN IN THAT SPACE WHERE SHADOW MEETS LIGHT... THAT BORDER-LAND OF DREAMS AND DEATH, AND DEATH AND LIFE.
NO DOOR IS CLOSED AGAINST US. NO SECRET CAN DEFY US. WE EXIST IN EVERY WORLD, EVERY UNIVERSE, EVERY POSSIBILITY. WE CANNOT BE DENIED, NOT EVEN BY THE DEAD.
WE ARE MAGNIFICENT, REN MORMORIAN. WE ARE FUCKING GLORIOUS.
AND NOW, BECAUSE OF YOUR *INCOMPETENCE* IN THE NORTH, THE SURVIVAL OF UBASTI'S CHILDREN IS NO LONGER ASSURED.
THERE IS NOW AN UNCERTAINTY. ONE THAT CANNOT BE TOLERATED.
NEKOMANCERS -- *NNNGH* -- HAVE *NEVER* ANSWERED TO THE POETS, AND THAT -- *MMMPH* -- WON'T START WITH ME.
MMPH!
NOR DID I COME HERE TO BE *LECTURED* OR *THREATENED.*
WHUMP
THE BLOOD OF THE SHAMAN-EMPRESS NO LONGER SLEEPS. THE OLD GOD HAS *AWAKENED.* I HEARD IT *SPEAK.*
AND THERE'S MORE.
YOU MUST TELL THE OTHERS.
THE PLAN *HAS* TO CHANGE.

GATHER ROUND, SAILORS!
WE'LL BE QUESTIONING YOU AND YOUR CAPTAINS OVER THE NEXT SEVERAL DAYS. ANOTHER BODY WAS JUST FOUND BY THE QUAY.
EATEN.
WHAT DO YOU MEAN, EATEN?
CUT OPEN, EVISCERATED.
NO ANIMAL DID IT. TOOK A PERSON TO MAKE THE INCISION. ATE JUST THE HEART AND LIVER, CHEWED ON OTHER BITS.
SECOND TIME THIS WEEK. WE HAVE A GHOUL KILLER IN OUR CITY.
YOU HEARD WHAT HAPPENED IN THE LIVESTOCK YARD, DIDN'T YOU? THERE WAS A GIRL CAUGHT FEEDING ON THE SHEEP. TORE 'EM OPEN WITH HER BARE HANDS, THEY SAY.
MISS? WAS IT YOU?
WILL ANYONE *COUGH* HELP US?

I'M WILLING TO WORK!
MY FATHER WAS A SOLDIER IN THE WAR...BUT THE WITCHES TOOK HIS LEGS...
PLEASE HELP.
MISS! WE HAVE TO --
SHUT UP. JUST... SHUT UP.
MISS, PLEASE. YOU MADE SO MUCH MONEY FROM SELLING SIR CORVIN'S SWIFT. CAN'T WE SPARE SOME?
SORRY, LITTLE FOX, BUT WE MIGHT NEED ALL OUR COIN BEFORE WE'RE THROUGH.
JUST BECAUSE YOU ARE AFRAID YOU WON'T HAVE ANYTHING TOMORROW DOESN'T MEAN YOU SHOULDN'T HELP PEOPLE TODAY.
WEREN'T YOU EVER HUNGRY AND ALONE? DIDN'T SOMEONE HELP YOU?
I'M *ALWAYS* HUNGRY, KIPPA.
KIPPA!
MASTER REN! YOU FOUND US!
BARELY IN TIME. WHAT ARE YOU BOTH DOING HERE?

DON'T YOU SEE THE CREST THOSE GUARDS ARE WEARING? IT'S THE MARK OF THE *BROTHERS IMURA.*
I KNOW. THEY CONTROL THE FISH MARKET. AND MORE.
ARE YOU CRAZY FOR TROUBLE?
THE BROTHERS IMURA ARE VILE FREEBOOTERS. NO ONE EVEN WHISPERS THEIR *NAMES,* FOR FEAR OF OFFENDING THE GODDESSES.
DO YOU KNOW WHAT IT TAKES TO BECOME AN EXILE OF ALL THE FAITHS?
THAT?
MEEP!
PRECISELY.
MISS?
YOU THREE.
COME WITH ME.

"HOW FAR WILL SHE SAIL?"
"TO THE FARTHEST SHORE, SIR. SHE'S BUILT FOR BOTH CAPACITY AND DISTANCE."
EASY ENOUGH TO CLAIM, BUT EVERY CREW THAT ATTEMPTS THE JOURNEY DIES OF THIRST OR HUNGER. THERE'S NO LAND TO THE EAST, MASTER-BUILDER. NOTHING CLOSE ENOUGH TO KEEP MY PEOPLE ALIVE. EVEN THE LATEST AIRSHIPS CAN'T MAKE THE JOURNEY.
THIS VESSEL IS DIFFERENT, SIR.
ITS SIZE IS DIRECTLY RELATED TO THE PROBLEM OF MAINTAINING THE CREW UNTIL THEY CAN REACH THE LOST CONTINENT. WE'VE FOUND A WAY TO BUILD COLD BOXES INTO THE LOWER --
MY APOLOGIES, MASTER-BUILDER. WE'LL HAVE TO CONTINUE THIS MEETING AN HOUR FROM NOW.
SOUFIAN, PLEASE ESCORT OUR GUEST TO THE CANTEEN. OUR BEST WINE FOR HER, PLEASE.

MAIKA HALFWOLF.
LOOK HOW YOU'VE GROWN.
AND WHAT AN OUTSTANDING KILLER YOU'VE BECOME.
IF THE WHISPERS I HEAR ARE TRUE.
THEY'RE TRUE, SEIZI.
YOU WERE JUST A CHILD THE LAST TIME I SAW YOU. DANCING IN THE STREET AT THE LUNAR FESTIVAL, WITH A SMILE SO BRIGHT EVEN *I* FELT WARMED. HOW YOU LOVED TO DANCE. SUCH A GOOD LITTLE WOLF.
AND NOW YOU'RE DEATH.
YOU ALSO BRING A FILTHY NEKOMANCER INTO MY HOUSE.
HE SMELLS LIKE A SNITCH. JUST LIKE THE REST OF HIS KIND. SQUEEZING THE DEAD TO GIVE UP THEIR SECRETS.
SUCH A TERRIBLE THING, NOT LEAVING GHOSTS TO THEIR PEACE.
LEAVE HIM ALONE!

I DON'T TRUST HIM, EITHER. BUT HE'S BEEN USEFUL. HE'LL BE LESS USEFUL IF KENZI UNTAILS HIM.
THERE'S NO ROOM AT SEA FOR ANYTHING LESS THAN ABSOLUTE LOYALTY. TRUST IS THE SAME AS BLOOD. THAT'S A LESSON YOUR MOTHER LEARNED TOO LATE.

OH, UBASTI, PLEASE.
LET US GO FOR A JAUNT, YOUNG WOLF, AND YOU CAN TELL ME WHY YOU'RE HERE.
BROTHER KENZI... FIND OUT WHAT YOU CAN FROM THE NEKOMANCER. MAKE SURE HE'S NOT HIDING ANYTHING. SAVE THE TAILS...FOR LATER.
MISS! STOP HIM!

HAVE YOUR GUARD TAKE THE LITTLE FOX OUT FOR LUNCH. SHE'S... SENTIMENTAL. AND IF ANYTHING HAPPENS TO HER... HE DIES.
PHYLLEAS? YOU LOOKING TO DIE?
NOT TODAY, BOSS.
NO, THIS IS WRONG! DON'T LET MASTER REN BE TORTURED!

HE BETRAYED ME TO THE DUSK COURT. YES OR NO?

I THOUGHT SO.
IT'S NOT RIGHT, MISS.

I'M GETTING SOFT. I MISS THE OCEAN, AND THE BLOOD. I SHOULD NEVER HAVE STOPPED PIRATING, BUT KENZI WASN'T THE SAME AFTER WHAT THE SEA FOLK DID TO HIM.
I CAN'T BE OUT THERE WITHOUT HIM. HE'S ALWAYS BEEN OUR LUCK.
BUT I SOOTHE MY LOSS WITH THE OBSCENE AMOUNTS OF COIN OUR LITTLE TRADE EMPIRE MAKES.

WITH THE BROTHERS IMURA, YOU HAVE A CREW, LITTLE WOLF. SMALL BUT LOYAL.

COME.

WHO HAS HELD YOU? WHO HAS HELD YOU SINCE YOUR MOTHER?

MAYBE ONE DAY YOU'LL REMEMBER THAT YOU HAD A LIFE BEFORE THE WAR.

IT'S FROM THE ISLE OF BONES. ONLY THOSE WITH A KEY CAN SURVIVE THAT ACCURSED ATOLL. YOUR MOTHER TOLD ME SHE LOST IT.
AND YOU KNOW ABOUT THIS KEY HOW? THE TRUTH NOW.

BECAUSE YOUR MOTHER WENT THERE. SEEKING ANSWERS.

FROM WHO?
NO ONE KNOWS WHAT POWER RULES THAT ISLE. YOUR MOTHER NEVER SPOKE OF HER JOURNEY.
YOU TOOK HER, DIDN'T YOU?
I WISH I'D REFUSED HER. MORIKO LOST SOMETHING OF HERSELF IN THAT PLACE. SURVIVING EXACTED A PRICE.
THERE WON'T BE ANYTHING LEFT OF ME IF I KEEP PAYING WHAT IT TAKES TO SURVIVE.
I'M RUNNING OUT OF TIME.
WHAT HAPPENED TO YOU, LITTLE WOLF? I HEAR THE WHISPERS, BUT IT'S HARD TO BELIEVE.
THE DUSK COURT IS HUNTING YOU. WITCHES ARE HUNTING YOU.

WILL YOU HELP ME OR NOT?

BOSS.
THYRIAN SOLDIERS HAVE ENTERED THE WAREHOUSE. THE BLOOD QUEEN IS WITH THEM. SHE SEEKS THE HALFWOLF.
THE BLOOD QUEEN? SHE KNOWS BETTER THAN TO COME HERE.
THE PACK THAT HUNTS YOU, WOLF, GROWS BIGGER.
PHYLLEAS! GET THE NEKOMANCER. BRING HIM TO THE JOLLY RAVAGER.
SO, YOUNG WOLF. IT APPEARS I'M GIVING YOU A SHIP, AFTER ALL.

THE JOLLY RAVAGER IS MY FINEST SHIP, AND HER CAPTAIN AND CREW ARE WITHOUT PEER. ALL OF THEM FOUGHT WITH ME IN THAT LAST BATTLE OF KEELSTONE REEF.
WHEN IT'S TIME TO MAKE THE BLASTED JOURNEY TO THE LOST CONTINENT, IT'LL BE THEM I WILL SAIL WITH. IF KENZI CAN BE PERSUADED, THAT IS.
MOVE YOUR ASSES! COMMANDER IMURA IS COMING ABOARD, AND WE NEED TO SET SAIL!
THE GULL SHOULD HAVE ALREADY RELAYED MY ORDERS, SYRYSSA.
I CAN'T SAY I'M PLEASED BY THE COURSE WE'RE SETTING. THAT'S BAD LUCK, SEIZI -- THE WAVE EMPRESS DOESN'T TAKE KINDLY TO HASTY FOOLS.
I'M THE FOOL. AND *I'M* ALSO THE REASON FOR THE HASTE.
THAT IS MORIKO HALFWOLF'S DAUGHTER.
WELL, WE *ARE* FUCKED, AREN'T WE?
LAUGH LATER. SHE'S BEING HUNTED BY THE CUMAEA *AND* THE DUSK COURT. WHICH MEANS *WE* ARE NOW BEING HUNTED.
THE BLOOD QUEEN HERSELF WANTS A WORD WITH MY GODDESS-DAUGHTER. I'LL FIND OUT WHETHER IT'S JUST WORDS, OR HER HEAD. BUT IN THE MEANTIME...
LET THEM ALL CHASE US.
I HAVE STARED INTO THE EYES OF THE WAVE EMPRESS, SEIZI. NOTHING ELSE CAN FRIGHTEN ME.

HERE, AND THEN GONE AGAIN. BUT THAT'S LIFE AT SEA.

YOU'LL BE MISSED. YOU'VE *BEEN* MISSED, ALL THESE YEARS. I HAD PLANS FOR YOU, YOUNG WOLF. YOU WERE GOING TO BE THE INHERITOR OF MY EMPIRE.

I'D TELL YOUR MOTHER THAT, AND SHE'D LAUGH. BUT I MEANT IT.

I...MISSED YOU, TOO. I JUST DIDN'T THINK...I COULD STAY. I WASN'T THE SAME AFTER THE WAR. I'M NOT THE SAME NOW. I'M... UNSAFE.

EVERYTHING I HAVE CAME FROM YEARS OF RUTHLESS MURDER. AM I SAFE? NO.

BUT I LOVE. I AM LOYAL. AND THAT IS MY REDEMPTION.

IF IT IS SO FOR ME...THEN WHY NOT YOU?

I DO SO LOVE WATCHING THE DEAD RISE.
WHAT A *TREAT.*

UBASTI OM DOMA. UBASTI OM AMOD.
SPEAK AS OUR LADY WARLORD COMMANDS...
...AND YOU SHALL BE FREED TO YOUR GODDESS FOR YOUR REBIRTH UPON THIS WORLD...OR ANOTHER.
...MURDERERS...
...YOU MURDERED US...
...YOU STOLE US FROM OUR LIVES...
...WHY...
...WHY...
...WHY...
CONSTANTINE.
YOU SURVIVED THE HEART OF THE BLAST.
TELL ME HOW.
YOU *MUST* ANSWER. THE SWORD OF THE EAST COMPELS YOU TO SPEAK.

...WE DON'T...
...KNOW HOW...
...WE SURVIVED...
...BUT WE KNOW...
...WHO SAVED US...
...MAIKA... HALFWOLF...
OH, MY.
MAIKA HALFWOLF?
THERE IS ONLY ONE HALFWOLF, LITTLE FOOLS, AND HER NAME IS *MORIKO.*
...YOU ARE... THE FOOL...
...MORIKO HAD... A *DAUGHTER*...
...A DAUGHTER... WHO WILL... REMAKE...
...THE WORLD...

WELL, THAT WAS AN ILLUMINATING CONVERSATION.

HOW WAS I UNAWARE THAT MORIKO HAD A CHILD?
HOW IS THAT *POSSIBLE?* MY SPIES... MY INFORMANTS... THEY *HAD* TO KNOW.
UNLESS...
PARDON ME, BUT PERHAPS YOU SHOULD FOCUS ON A *DIFFERENT* QUESTION?

WE THOUGHT THE WEAPON THAT DESTROYED CONSTANTINE WAS A... *THING.*
NOW... IT SEEMS IT IS A PERSON. NOT JUST *ANY* PERSON, EITHER.

THE DUSK COURT -- *MMPH* -- RECENTLY BROKE ITS SILENCE AND BATTLED THE CUMAEA SOUTH OF ZAMORA, NEAR THE WALL. A BATTLE THAT *POSSIBLY* RESULTED IN A -- *CRNCH* -- LOCALIZED BLAST OF INFERNAL ENERGY.

PERHAPS OUR RIVALS ARE ONE STEP AHEAD.
THEY MIGHT ALREADY HAVE THE GIRL... WHICH BODES ILL FOR US.

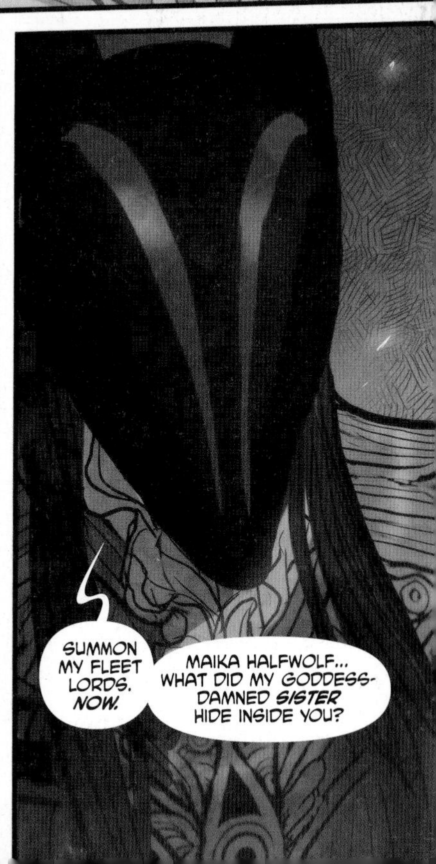
MAIKA HALFWOLF... WHAT DID MY GODDESS-DAMNED *SISTER* HIDE INSIDE YOU?
SUMMON MY FLEET LORDS. *NOW.*

An excerpt of a lecture from the esteemed **Professor Tam Tam**, former First Record-Keeper of the Is'hami Temple, and learned contemporary of Namron Black Claw...

CHAPTER EIGHT

Mother...
...I thought all that mattered was finding answers about your death....
...but it turns out your life is what I should have been hunting all along.
NO! LET GO! LET GO!
You sailed these very seas when you went searching for your answers...
THE CREW IS BACK FROM THE WELL STATION, CAPTAIN. ALL THE DRINKING WATER IS ABOARD.
GOOD, JAN. TIME WE HAD THE WIND BEHIND OUR SAILS.
I HAD A DREAM LAST NIGHT WE WERE BEING WATCHED, AND THAT DREAM ENDED IN BLOOD.
SEA DREAMS ARE NOT TO BE IGNORED, CAPTAIN. THOUGH WHAT THEY MEAN ONLY THE POETS CAN KNOW FOR CERTAIN.
...now I'm here chasing after you.
HELP!
ARE YOU SURE THIS IS SAFE FOR THE CHILD, HALFWOLF?
SOME SAILORS SAY IT'S BEST NOT TO LEARN HOW TO SWIM, BUT I'D RATHER SHE HAVE A FIGHTING CHANCE WHILE WE'RE AT SEA.
OF COURSE, BUT COULDN'T YOU HAVE SELECTED SOMEONE LESS... SHARKISH... TO BE HER TEACHER?
YOU'D BE WISE NOT TO DISPARAGE OUR CREW, CAT.

Even though you're dead, there's a part of me that believes maybe I'll find you.

YOU MIGHT NOT LIKE WHAT HAPPENS.

HSSST!

The truth is...all I'll ever find is your ghost. But for someone like me...a ghost is better than nothing.

I AM SICK TO ***DEATH*** OF BEING THREATENED BY MONGREL TIGER-KIN. PUT ANOTHER CLAW IN MY FACE, AND I'LL HAVE IT FOR A NECKLACE!

THANK YOU FOR TRYING TO TEACH ME SWIMMING, MISS... OLD TOOTH.
I'M SORRY I JUMPED WHEN I FIRST SAW YOU. THAT WAS VERY RUDE.
YOU HAD NO REASON TO KNOW I AM AN ARCANIC. YOU LANDERS HAVE BEEN DRY SO LONG YOU'VE FORGOTTEN THE FACES OF YOUR SEA SISTERS AND BROTHERS.
JAN, LEAVE THE NEKOMANCER ALONE. HE MIGHT ENSLAVE YOUR GHOST AFTER YOU DIE.
HE'LL NEED TO GROW A FEW EXTRA TAILS IF HE WANTS TO TAKE *MY* SOUL, CAPTAIN.
RAISE THE ANCHOR! RIXA, THE SAILS!
MASTER REN! DID YOU SEE ME DROWNING?
YES.
KIPPA.
I DID.
MISS! MISS! I WAS IN THE SEA!
YOU, HALFPUP. I HEARD THE WAY YOU TALKED TO THE CAPTAIN JUST NOW. THAT WON'T DO.
NOT FROM A *HUMAN.* NOT FROM *ANYONE.*
I'M AS ARCANIC AS YOU.
THAT'S PLENTY RICH. YOU'RE GONNA NEED MORE THAN A *DROP* OF TRUE BLOOD TO MAKE YOU ONE OF US.

Mother...
Thyrians were always famous for their tolerance, but the war has made them hard. The war made us all hard.
RIGHT NOW YOU SMELL LIKE A DIRTY HUMAN. YOU LOOK LIKE A DIRTY HUMAN.
THAT MAKES YOU A DIRTY HUMAN.
SMAK!
They don't trust people who look like me anymore....
AND YOU, A DIRTY HUMAN LOVER...
Changelings, they call us. Traitors.
CALL ME DIRTY...OR HUMAN... AGAIN.
FUCK...OFF... BACK TO THE... WITCHES...
MISS, NO!
Do you remember when I was small? How I wanted to have Goddess-marks like the other Arcanic children?

I wanted a wolf tail. I wanted wolf claws and wolf teeth.
AIEEEE!
SHLUCK!
Do you remember what you said?
"Little wolf, you have all those things. But they are safe within you, where no one can take them.
WHAM!
ERRGH..
"Sometimes, my darling...it's better to hide your teeth."
FUCK... FUCK...
Easy enough for you, mother...but hiding was never easy for me.
ANYONE ELSE WANT TO ARGUE?

HA! HAHAHA!
HOW FUNNY IS THE BLOOD? HOW FUNNY OF YOU ALL TO TRY TO COW THE HALFWOLF.
YOU, MAIKA.
IF YOU HURT MY CREW AGAIN, YOU'LL PAY WITH YOUR LIFE.
THE REST OF YOU...DEFY MY ORDER OF PROTECTION, AND I'LL BE THE ONE DOING THE DISMEMBERING.
STOP CRYING. IT'LL GROW BACK.
SOME OF US AREN'T THAT LUCKY.
I ASSUME YOU CAN CLIMB AS WELL AS YOU CAN FIGHT.

NNNGH.
A SHIP IS A VERY FRAGILE THING.

COMMANDER IMURA USED TO SAY THAT YOU HAVE TO BE HARDER THAN STEEL TO HOLD A SHIP TOGETHER.
AND HERE YOU ARE, TRYING TO TEAR MY SHIP TO SPLINTERS.
THE COMMANDER ASKED ME TO BRING YOU TO THE ISLE OF BONES, BUT WHAT I'M TEMPTED TO DO IS JUST BLEED YOU AND THROW YOUR BODY TO THE DEEP. MAKE AN EXCUSE TO THE OLD MAN.

BUT THEY'RE SENTIMENTAL... AND THEY'VE LOST ENOUGH.

SAVE YOUR LECTURES, CAPTAIN, FOR PEOPLE WHO HAVE TO LISTEN TO THEM.
YOU DON'T NEED TO LIKE ME. YOU JUST HAVE TO OBEY.
I'VE MET YOUR KIND, HALFWOLF. YOU THINK YOU CAN TAKE PIECES OF PEOPLE, AND THERE WON'T BE CONSEQUENCES.

IT'S THOSE LIKE YOU WHO SINK SHIPS. BUT I'LL TELL YOU ONE THING: YOU WON'T SINK *MINE.*

THE SEA TEACHES THERE ARE CONSEQUENCES TO EVERYTHING.
EVERYTHING, YOU HEAR? SMALL RIPPLES BECOME WAVES THAT CAN RAVAGE EVEN THE SAFEST HARBOR.

WHEN YOUR WAVE COMES... I DON'T THINK YOU'RE GOING TO LOOK SO BRAVE.

YOU'LL NEED MORE THAN YOUR HANDS TO SCRUB AWAY THAT MESS.
DID ANY BLOOD GET IN YOUR EYES?
NO, MA'AM.
HOW IS MISS?
SAVE YOUR CONCERN, GIRL. YOU THINK YOU CAN ACCOMPANY HER... BUT LET ME GIVE YOU A LESSON: SHARKS SWIM ALONE.
ONE DAY SHE'S GOING TO EAT YOU. BELIEVE ME.
YOU ARE WELCOME TO STAY HERE, IF YOU WANT. I COULD TURN YOU INTO A SAILOR.
BESIDES, FOXES ALWAYS BRING GOOD LUCK.
BUT I BELIEVE IN MISS MAIKA.
THAT'S NOT THE PROBLEM.
THE PROBLEM IS THAT SHE DOESN'T BELIEVE IN YOU.
WHEN SHE'S ANGRY... DO YOU THINK YOU EVEN EXIST?

JAN...OLD TOOTH...I WANTED YOU BOTH TO HEAR IT FIRST.
WE'RE SAILING FOR THE ISLE OF BONES.
OF *COURSE* WE ARE.
FIGURED THAT WAS WHERE THE COMPASS WAS POINTING, CAPTAIN.
COULDN'T RECKON ANOTHER REASON THE HALFWOLF'S DAUGHTER WOULD BE ON OUR SHIP.

THE CREW WILL PROTEST, TO PUT IT MILDLY.

WHAT CAN YOU TELL US ABOUT THE ISLAND?
I SAW VERY LITTLE. I STAYED WITH THE LAUNCH. I REMEMBER AN IMMENSE, CURVED WALL THAT LOOKED LIKE IT HAD BEEN MADE FROM A LEVIATHAN'S RIBS.
LADY HALFWOLF AND COMMANDER IMURA WERE THE ONLY ONES TO GO ASHORE INTO THE MISTS. BUT THEY NEVER SPOKE OF WHAT THEY SAW.

EIGHTEEN YEARS AGO YOU WOULD HAVE BEEN A CHILD.
JAN WAS INDEED A CUB -- SNUCK ABOARD OUR SKIFF, AGAINST ORDERS. THE COMMANDER NEARLY BEAT THE STRIPES OUT OF HIS FUR FOR THAT.
I HAD TO SEE FOR MYSELF WHAT WAS MAKING YOU ADULTS PISS YOUR BREECHES. IT WASN'T ALL THAT BAD.

CUT THAT LYING TONGUE. I'VE SAILED MANY A DARK SEA, BUT THOSE MISTS ARE SOME OF THE DARKEST.
I'D RATHER NOT GO BACK INSIDE THAT ABYSS.
DON'T BE SO *GLOOMY,* SWEET FIN.
STOP YOUR PLAYING, JAN.

YOU DON'T UNDERSTAND, MISS. YOU CANNOT NAVIGATE IN THAT PLACE. IT'S A WHITE VEIL THAT COMES DOWN BETWEEN YOU AND THE WORLD.
ALL YOU DO IS ROW AND PRAY THE WAVE EMPRESS WILL GUIDE YOU TO LAND.
AND THAT'S NOT ACCOUNTING FOR THE SCREAMS.
SCREAMS?
THE POETS SAY THAT THOSE WHO NEVER MAKE IT TO LAND ARE TRAPPED IN THE MIST FOR ALL ETERNITY.

WE'LL SEND IN A TWO-PERSON SKIFF. JUST THE HALFWOLF AND ONE OTHER TO MAKE THE LANDING AND MIND THE CRAFT WHILE SHE GOES ASHORE.

I DON'T NEED ANYONE ELSE. I CAN DO IT ON MY OWN.
THEN YOU *ARE* A FOOL. YOU'RE NOT GOING BY YOURSELF. YOU NEED SOMEONE WHO CAN HELP NAVIGATE YOU TO SHORE.
OLD TOOTH SAID IT AMOUNTS TO LITTLE MORE THAN *PRAYING* YOU'RE HEADED IN THE RIGHT DIRECTION. WHY DO I NEED ANOTHER PERSON FOR THAT?
I'LL KNOW WHERE LAND IS.

I'LL SMELL IT, MISS. EVEN IF THE AIR IS BAD.
I KNOW I WILL.

YOU ARE STAYING ON THIS BOAT, KIPPA. ELDRITCH FOG IS BEST LEFT TO THE ONES WHO DON'T KNOW BETTER.
FOR ONCE, I AGREE WITH THE CAT.

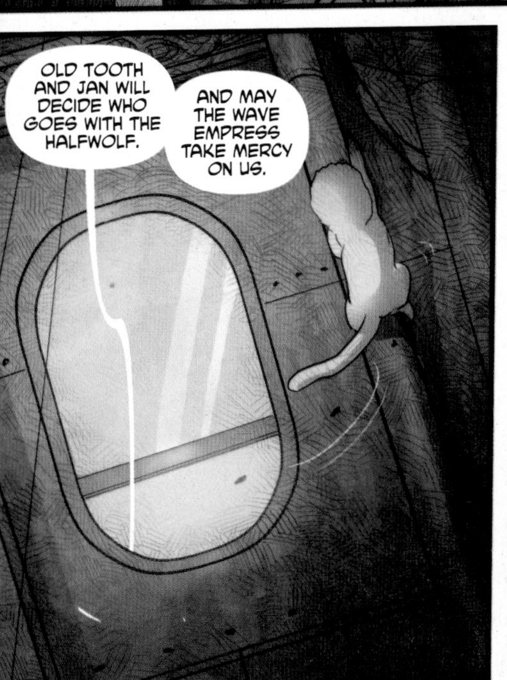
OLD TOOTH AND JAN WILL DECIDE WHO GOES WITH THE HALFWOLF.
AND MAY THE WAVE EMPRESS TAKE MERCY ON US.

IT IS AS OUR MASTER SUSPECTED...

OUR ORDERS ARE TO PREVENT THE HALFWOLF FROM LANDING ON THAT ISLAND.
AND HOW WILL WE STOP HER? SHE IS TOO STRONG. YOU SAW HOW SHE TORE THE LIMB OFF THE SEA-BREED.
HOW YOUNG YOU BOTH ARE. THERE ARE WAYS, I ASSURE YOU.
AND WHEN THE HALFWOLF IS DEAD?
WE WILL ALSO TAKE THE MASK.

FUCK.
YOU'RE BACK.

YOU HAVE... BEEN UNWISE...
...THE SEA SLAYS AS MANY AS IT CARRIES... HERE, DEATH IS EVERYWHERE.
...DEATH FOR YOU... REBIRTH FOR ME.

YOU ATE THE REST OF MY ARM, YOU SISTER-FUCKER. THAT WASN'T PART OF THE BARGAIN WHEN I GAVE YOU YOUR NAME.
NO... YOU ATE IT... YOURSELF...

...JUST AS YOU ATE... THE FIRST TIME... YOU WOKE ME...
...YOU CANNOT SUMMON... THAT MUCH POWER... WITHOUT A PRICE...

IMAGINE... WHAT YOU MIGHT LOSE... THE NEXT TIME YOU DECIDE... TO TAKE CONTROL?

WHY ARE WE... AT SEA... CHILD...? THE WAVES DO NOT FAVOR MY KIND.

I HAVE A DIFFERENT QUESTION, MONSTER.

DO YOU KNOW WHAT THE FUCK THIS IS?

WHERE... DID YOU FIND... THAT ACCURSED PIECE... OF BONE?
THAT DOESN'T MATTER.
OF COURSE... IT MATTERS... WHEN WHAT YOU ARE HOLDING... IS FROM THE SKELETON... OF A GOD...

YOU ONLY WANT TO KEEP *YOURSELF* SAFE.

IT IS WISE...TO CARE...ABOUT SURVIVAL...ONLY A FOOL...INVITES THEIR OWN... RUIN...

...WHICH IS WHY... I FIND YOUR USUAL LACK OF SELF-PRESERVATION... SO UNUSUAL...

...I WILL LIVE...A WHILE LONGER...

...AND NOT EVEN THE SPECTER...OF A GOOD DROWNING...

...WILL KEEP ME...FROM MY APPETITES...

There was always the possibility that things might have turned out differently.
Some Arcanics only get the mark when they're of age. Then, their eyes change, or their teeth grow sharp... or their tails appear.
...THEY WILL NEVER KNOW...
...OR MAKE A SOUND...
...AND THEIR BODIES... WILL BE EASILY DISCARDED...
I prayed to the goddess. I prayed for anything-- any mark would do.
MISS, NO. YOU CAN'T FEED ON THE SAILORS. YOU JUST CAN'T.
YES, CONTROL THAT THING. FOR ALL OUR SAKES.
I should have listened to the poets: "Be careful what you desire," they say.
...HA... HA... HA...
YES... CHILD... CONTROL ME...
I should have listened to you, mother.
...CONTROL... OUR HUNGER...

NO!

...THAT... IS NOT WHAT I HAD... IN MIND...

SPLSSH

MISS! SOMEONE HELP!

FUCK. ME.

GASP!

YOU... ARE SUCH... A BOTHER...

GO AND DIE HUNGRY.

OH, CHILD... I AM NOTHING... IF NOT... RESOURCEFUL...

NO!

...YES... THIS WILL... SATISFY...
...THOUGH THE PRESENCE... OF A SIREN... IS QUITE STRANGE...
HSSSSSHSSS
...IT CANNOT BE AN ACCIDENT... THAT SHE WAS SO CLOSE...TO THE SHIP.
IT SEEMS... ALL THE POWERS... ARE WAKING...

GASP
IT HASN'T BEEN LONG. SHE MIGHT STILL BE ALIVE.
OR PERHAPS SHE'S ALREADY GONE.
TRIM THE SAILS! PREPARE THE LAUNCH.
NO NEED.
MISS!
WHAT GAME ARE YOU PLAYING, HALFWOLF?
DO YOU WANT TO DIE?
IT WOULD BE EASIER.

MISS... STOP.
LIVING ISN'T SUPPOSED TO BE EASY. IF IT WAS EASY IT WOULDN'T BE CALLED LIFE. SO SAY THE POETS.
ALSO, THE GODDESS TELLS US HOW WE'RE REBORN REFLECTS HOW WE LIVE IN THIS LIFE... AND YOU'RE FIGHTING TO BE BETTER, MISS. YOU JUST THREW YOURSELF OFF THE SHIP TO KEEP THE MONSTER FROM HURTING ANYONE.
IS THAT WHY I TRIED TO DROWN MYSELF, LITTLE FOX?
ALSO, YOUR GODDESS CAN EAT SHIT.
WHAT MAKES YOU THINK I'M NOT ALREADY PAYING FOR CRIMES FROM ANOTHER LIFE?
OR MAYBE I'M THE ONE MAKING EVERYONE ELSE PAY. MAYBE I WAS SUPPOSED TO BE AN AWFUL PERSON... TO HELP THE GODDESS BALANCE HER SCALES.
NO, MISS.
YOU'RE NOT AWFUL.
ACTUALLY, YOU'RE REALLY FUCKED UP.
GET ME SOMETHING TO DRY OFF WITH, LITTLE FOX.
BOOM!

From the archives of the esteemed **Professor Tam Tam**, former First Record-Keeper of the Is'hami Temple, and learned contemporary of Namron Black Claw...

THE FEDERATION NEEDS YOU!

The liberty and safety of every human is under dire threat. The liberty and safety of every human is under dire threat. The liberty and safety of every human is under dire threat.

The liberty and safety of every human is under dire threat. Won't you be the hero we need?

Answer the call. Won't you be the hero we need?

Visit your local government office or Cumaean house of worship and band together with your comrad

JOIN NOW

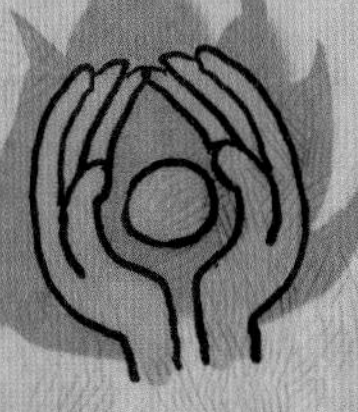

IF THE FEDERATION FALLS, YOU FA

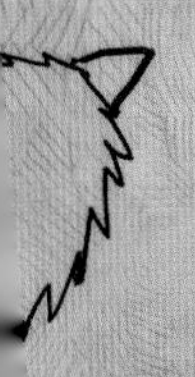

HURRY!
OVER... HERE...
I SEE THEM!
HALFWOLF! ANSWER ME, DAMN YOU!
FUCK.

KNOW YOUR ENEMY!
DEMONICAS are the most terrible and ancient of the demons who threaten humankind. Immortal, hungry for flesh, they keep harems of tortured humans – and forcibly breed upon them the living atrocities that we know as...
...HALF-SPAWNS. Part human, part Demonica – all fiend. When young, their strength is limited – but at puberty the Half-Spawn experiences the Awakening, and gains their power.
Beware the DECEIVERS, Half-Spawn who can pass as human. Never let down your guard! Test even the most innocent face with a dog or scope!
DESTROY THESE MAD BRUTES!
ENLIST TODAY!

CHAPTER NINE

WHY YES...
...I MOST CERTAINLY PREVENTED YOU AND YOUR SPIES FROM DISCOVERING YOUR SISTER HAD A CHILD.
YOU'RE A FOOL IF YOU THINK I'D DO LESS THAN PROTECT MY ONLY LIVING GRANDCHILD FROM YOUR... IMPULSES.
YOU THOUGHT I WOULD MURDER MY OWN NIECE.

MY DARLING SWORD OF THE EAST...
...PERHAPS YOU WOULDN'T HAVE MURDERED HER OUTRIGHT... BUT YOU WOULD HAVE HELD THE CHILD HOSTAGE AND BROKEN HER LITTLE BODY TO PIECES... IF IT MEANT MAKING MORIKO OBEY.
AND MORIKO WOULD *NOT* HAVE OBEYED. BOTH OF YOU ARE THE SAME, IN THAT REGARD.
YOU DECAYING BITCH. ALL THESE YEARS YOU PROTECTED HER SECRETS.
YOU KNEW, DIDN'T YOU, THAT MORIKO HAD FOUND THE WEAPON I'VE BEEN SEARCHING FOR. THE WEAPON THAT COULD SAVE US.
THE WEAPON THAT WILL DESTROY US, YOU MEAN.
YOU AND MORIKO WERE BOTH WRONG TO SEARCH FOR THAT...THING. IF THE SHAMAN-EMPRESS HERSELF DEEMED HER CREATION TOO DANGEROUS TO CONTROL, THEN WHAT DAMNED HUBRIS ALLOWED YOU TO THINK THAT YOU WERE UP TO THE TASK?
BETTER ME THAN THE DUSK COURT. OR THE FEDERATION OF MAN AND THEIR WITCHES.
SAID LIKE A MORTAL CHILD.
THE WEAPON YOU SEEK IS NOT WHAT YOU THINK IT IS.
YOU WILL NEVER CONTROL IT. YOU CAN ONLY STALL ITS ARRIVAL, AND EVEN THAT IS FUTILE. A YEAR OR TEN THOUSAND... WHAT SLEEPS MUST AWAKEN.

HOW IT AWAKENS, HOWEVER... AND WHO DOES THE WAKING...
NOW THAT MIGHT MAKE ALL THE DIFFERENCE BETWEEN MOST DEAD... AND ALL DEAD.
BUT YOU, MY DEAR, ARE MOSTLY IRRELEVANT TO EITHER OUTCOME.
YOU TALK LIKE THIS WEAPON IS A LIVING THING. IT'S JUST A MASK.
AND NOW THE DUSK COURT HAS BROKEN ITS SILENCE. THEY FOUND MORIKO'S DAUGHTER... AND SURELY THE WEAPON MY SISTER GAVE HER.
MY POOR DEAR. HOW LITTLE YOU KNOW.
I SUPPOSE I PUT YOU AT A DISADVANTAGE WHEN I BOUGHT ALL YOUR SPIES. YOUR BRILLIANCE I'M AFRAID, DOES NOT EXTEND FAR BEYOND THE BATTLEFIELD.
IF ONLY YOUR SISTER WAS STILL ALIVE.
THIS IS HER FAULT, AFTER ALL.
YOU --
NO, YOU WILL NOT SPEAK.
AN ENVOY OF THE DUSK COURT IS COMING HERE TO DISCUSS HOW WE MIGHT ALLY OURSELVES IN OUR COMMON GOAL OF CONTAINING THIS... WEAPON... YOU SO DESIRE.
IN FACT, I BELIEVE SHE'S ALREADY ARRIVED. SO DO BE POLITE. SHE KNOWS MORE ABOUT MORIKO'S DAUGHTER THAN ANYONE ALIVE.

THE BARONESS OF THE LAST DUSK.
WELCOME TO THE DAWN COURT.

There are some things I wish I could forget. You know what they are, Mother.
...MEMORIES... SLIPPING AWAY FROM ME...
You would call me ungrateful. And maybe...you would be right.
I'm alive, after all.
...WHAT... ARE YOU...SUPPOSED TO BE...?
...YOU... LOOK... FAMILIAR...
That's all that ever mattered to you.
...NOT THAT I HAVE... ANY PRIVACY...TO REMEMBER...
I always told myself you wanted me to survive because you loved me...
SHUT YOUR EYES. NOW.
Now I doubt love had anything to do with it.
AND TELL ME HOW YOU WOULD KILL SOMEONE.

Who are you to me, really?
YOU HAVE THIRTY SECONDS.

THE PEN. I COULD STAB SOMEONE IN THE EYES OR THROAT.
And who am I...

THIS COULD BREAK SOMEONE'S FACE. CRUSH SKULLS, SMASH BRAINS.
...if not even you loved me...

THE BOOKS... I COULD THROW THEM? MAYBE THE... THE INK...
...if I was just part of a plan...

...a vision...
YOU'RE NOT THINKING. SEE THAT SCARF? DO YOU?
WHAT CAN YOU DO WITH IT AFTER YOU'VE DISABLED YOUR OPPONENT?
GASP
I DON'T KNOW!
THUNK

THAT IS NOT AN ACCEPTABLE ANSWER.
...an outcome...

...that you manipulated into existence?
YOU NEED TO UNDERSTAND WHAT THIS FEELS LIKE... WHAT IT'S CAPABLE OF DOING...
S-STOP! MOMMY GAK PLEASE!
...PERHAPS THEN YOU WON'T FORGET IT'S A TOOL TO BE USED...

Who am I, Mother?
WHAT IS GOING ON IN HERE?
JUST A LESSON, SEIZI.
SOUNDED MORE LIKE A BEATING.
MAIKA HAS BEEN LAZY OF LATE. I'M TEACHING HER HOW TO FOCUS.
After the war I forgot myself...
IS THAT SO? BY HURTING HER?
...except that I was your daughter...
I WASN'T HURTING HER. DO YOU FEEL ANY PAIN, MAIKA? DO YOU FEEL ANY FEAR?
NO, MOMMY.
...and now that is no comfort.
YOU FEAR FOR MAIKA'S SURVIVAL -- I UNDERSTAND THAT. WE ALL KNOW A WAR IS COMING.
BUT THERE ARE OTHER WAYS TO PREPARE A CHILD THAN --
THIS IS NOT ABOUT THE WAR.
SHE NEEDS TO PREPARE FOR WHO SHE WILL BECOME.
I want to please you. Even dead, you own me.
YOU'VE SEEN SOMETHING WITH YOUR SIGHT.
I KNOW HER ANCESTRY.
SHE'S A WOLF, LIKE YOU.
THAT'S THE PROBLEM. SHE HAS TO BE BETTER THAN ME. STRONGER.
STRONGER THAN ANY OF US.
But what will be the price?
HOW UNFORTUNATE... YOU DID NOT BECOME... THE DAUGHTER YOUR MOTHER... DESIRED...
YES, UNFORTUNATE.
What do I have to give up of myself to be worthy of your ghost?
LET'S SEE IF YOU CAN BE USEFUL.
WAKE UP. NOW.

HALFWOLF! STOP!
WHAT... NOW...? AND WHY... ARE YOU INJURED?
THE MASK AND KEY WERE STOLEN. CAN YOU SENSE WHERE THEY ARE?
FOOLISH GIRL... I WARNED YOU...
CAN YOU DO IT?
...CAN YOU NOT... HEAR... THAT HUM...?
BELOW US...
I THOUGHT THAT WAS MY STOMACH.
GODDESS...
OLD TOOTH! GET THE HALFWOLF BEFORE THOSE INJURIES KILL HER!

WE MUST HURRY.
CAPTAIN WILL BE CALLING FOR THE ENTIRE CREW AFTER THE BLAST. DAMNED SHORT TRICK COULD HAVE WARNED US. HE BETTER HAVE KILLED THE GIRL.
ALL THIS TROUBLE TO KEEP THE HALFWOLF AWAY FROM THE ISLE OF BONES.
OUR MASTER SHOULD HAVE DESTROYED MORIKO ALL THOSE YEARS AGO, BEFORE HER DAUGHTER COULD BE BORN.
BUT HE WAS TOO AFRAID.
CAREFUL. SHORT TRICK WILL HEAR YOU AND TELL HIM. WHAT THE MONKEY HEARS, OUR MASTER HEARS.
YOU WON'T GET A NEW BODY -- AND THAT ONE IS ALREADY DYING AROUND YOU.
BAH. WE'LL SMUGGLE THESE RELICS STRAIGHT INTO HIS HANDS. HE'LL BE TOO PLEASED TO DENY US FRESH SKINS.
THEY SAY... TOUCHING THE MASK GIVES YOU A GLIMPSE OF THE OTHER SIDE. THAT YOU CAN HEAR THE VOICE.
DON'T BE A FOOL... THAT'S NOT MEANT FOR US. WE MUST SERVE. WE MUST OBEY. NEVER FORGET THAT.
WHO WOULD KNOW? AND IF THE DOOR WERE TO OPEN... IF WE WERE THE ONES TO FREE OUR GODS...
...DON'T PRETEND YOU CAN'T ALREADY HEAR THE WHISPER...
IGNORE IT...
...IT'S THE FIRST SONG... THE SUSURRUS OF DEFILING...
I... HEAR ...SWEET BLASPHEMIES...
...BUT YOU... WILL SING IT... NOT.
SPLAT!

GREATEST DESTROYER... YOU...YOU ARE RISEN!
BASE VERMIN...YOU DARE...CONSPIRE... AGAINST MY HOST...SWIFT COMES...YOUR ANNIHILATION...
FORGIVE US, MASTER OF WOES!
WE WOULD NEVER...NEVER HAVE DARED IF WE'D KNOWN!
OH...HOW I DESPISE... UNTRUTHS...
WHAT IS THIS THING? ONE OF YOU?
...AS A WORM...IS TO YOU... PERHAPS...
...IT IS A RELIC... FROM OUR DAYS OF FREEDOM...SHADOWS THAT ONCE SERVED US...IN HUNTING MORTALS...DURING THE WAR...
...WE WOULD GIVE THEM...BODIES IN REWARD...BUT THEY WERE SPITEFUL...FULL OF ENVY... ALWAYS DESIRING MORE... THAN THEIR PLACE...
WHO SENT YOU? WAS IT THE CREATURE WHO LIVES INSIDE THE WITCH?
TELL ME!
W-WHAT WITCH?
I CAN'T... I... G-G-GAAK-K-K...
FOOL... A COMPULSION HAS BEEN...PLACED UPON IT...
...SUCH WEAK CREATURES... SO EASILY CONTROLLED...
HEAR ME, DESTROYER! DO NOT GO TO THAT ISLAND! YOUR DIVINE LIFE WILL BE IN DANGER! THE LORD OF CARRION WILL TRAP YOU. HE WILL USE YOU TO ESCAPE HIS CHAINS --
I CANNOT BE USED...BY ANYONE...
WHY DO YOU KNOW MY MOTHER'S NAME?
SHE WAS KNOWN -- ≠KKGAK≠ -- TO OUR MASTER...
MAIKA! I KNOW YOU'RE DOWN THERE!
FUCK.

OH, UBASTI. DELIVER US.
A RIFT FIEND... HERE... AND FREE...
KILL... KILL -- KILL!
YOU'LL DIE FIRST, HOUND.
SNARL!
URK!
THIS... GROWS... WEARISOME...
KILL IT, HALFWOLF!
YOU'VE SEEN THIS CREATURE BEFORE?
OUR MOST ANCIENT ENEMY? OF COURSE I HAVE.
IN THE TEMPLE IN ARKANGELUS THERE'S A ROOM WHERE WE KEEP THEIR HEADS PICKLED IN JARS.
UBASTI'S SOLDIERS IMPRISONED THE RIFT HOUNDS AFTER THE GREAT WAR OF THE GODS... BUT THEY ALWAYS FIND WAYS OF ESCAPING.
WHAT HAVE YOU DONE? WE NEEDED TO KEEP QUESTIONING THAT THING!
...TO WHAT... PURPOSE...? IT HAD REACHED... THE END... OF ITS UTILITY...
IT KNEW WHAT WAS WAITING FOR US ON THE ISLAND --

WHERE THE FUCK ARE YOU GOING?
YOU... FOUND... THE MASK... THE INSURRECTION HAS BEEN... SUPPRESSED...
...AND I WAS OCCUPIED... WHEN YOU... INTRUDED...
...YOU ARE NOT... THE ONLY ONE... WHO MUST REMEMBER...
CAT...WHO COULD CONTROL THESE... RIFT HOUNDS?
NOT EVEN OUR GREATEST WAS ABLE TO COMMAND THEM.
THE SHAMAN-EMPRESS WAS SAID TO HAVE HAD THAT POWER... BUT WHETHER THAT WAS DUE TO HER OWN GIFTS OR AN INVENTION, I CANNOT SAY.
CAN YOU DETECT THEM?
NOT EASILY.
THEY ENTER BODIES LIKE A GHOST... AND THEN BECOME FLESH AS THEY CONSUME THEIR HOST.
THOSE RIFT FIENDS SPOKE OF A LORD OF CARRION... THAT HE WAITS ON THE ISLAND TO TRAP THE MONSTER... TO TRAP *US.*
DO YOU KNOW THIS DEMON?
I HAVE NOT HEARD THAT EPITHET BEFORE. IT DOES NOT SOUND EXACTLY WELCOMING.
NO, IT FUCKING DOES NOT.

WHAT WERE YOU DOING IN THAT HOLD?
I WAS SEARCHING FOR WHOEVER TRIED TO KILL ME.
THE CAPTAIN IS ROUNDING UP THE CREW EVEN NOW. WE'LL GET ANSWERS SOON ENOUGH.
YOU'RE SERIOUSLY WOUNDED, LASS. IT'S A MIRACLE YOU HAVEN'T COLLAPSED ALREADY FROM THE BLOOD LOSS -- OR THE PAIN.
I BARELY FEEL IT.

IS IT ALL THE HALFWOLF'S BLOOD?
SOME, NOT ALL. THERE'S A FOUL STENCH, TOO.
GILLY AND MAGDA. WE JUST PICKED THEM UP IN THYRIA...CAME RECOMMENDED FROM THE BLOOD QUEEN'S OWN FLEET.
BUT YOU DIDN'T SCENT THEM IN THE HALFWOLF'S CABIN?
COULDN'T SAY. TOO MUCH SMOKE FOR MY NOSE.

YEARS AGO, I SAW A TOOTH LIKE THIS IN MY DREAMS. THE FACE THAT BORE IT WAS INFERNAL.
BACK THEN I WAS BED-HOPPING WITH A CUMAEAN SCIENTIST WHO WAS OBSESSED WITH THOSE OLD GODS. I BLAMED THE DREAMS ON HER. SOMETIMES A WITCH'S THOUGHTS LEAK.

ROUND UP THE NEW SAILORS. QUESTION THEM FIRMLY. I DON'T HAVE TIME FOR LIES.
AND GET AN OLD-TIMER WITH A HOOK DOWN HERE FOR A POKE-AROUND -- SEE IF ANY BODIES ARE FOUND IN THE CHUTE.

AND THE HALFWOLF? WHAT I SAW COMING OUT OF HER STUMP... IT SCARED ME.
THEN *I'M* SCARED
BUT TOMORROW SHE GOES TO THE ISLE OF BONES. IF WE'RE LUCKY, THAT'S THE LAST WE'LL EVER SEE OF HER.

PLEASE FORGIVE MY LATENESS, BUT THERE WAS ANOTHER MURDER NEAR OUR WAREHOUSE. THE GHOUL KILLER, THEY CALL HIM...GIVEN THE STATE OF THE CORPSE.
BUT DO TRY THIS WHISKEY FROM GRIM HAVEN. I'M TOLD IT CAN MAKE A DARK WORLD BRIGHT.
THE LAST TIME WE DRANK TOGETHER, MORIKO WAS PREPARING FOR HER GREAT EXPEDITION.
NOW HER DAUGHTER HAS RETURNED. AND WITH HER, TROUBLE. WITH THE HALFWOLFS, IT IS ALWAYS TROUBLE.
SOMETIMES THAT'S THE PRICE OF FRIENDSHIP.

A PRICE MY PEOPLE CAN NO LONGER AFFORD...THYRIA WAS ALMOST LOST DURING THE WAR, SEIZI.
IT WILL BE ANOTHER GENERATION BEFORE WE REGAIN OUR FORMER STRENGTH, BUT WE DON'T HAVE THE LUXURY OF TIME. WE NEED WEAPONS, ALLIANCES...AND WE NEED THEM NOW.
WAR WITH THE FEDERATION IS COMING. THE WITCHES ARE COMING. FOR OUR LAND, FOR THE LILIUM IN OUR BONES.

BUT PERHAPS WE HAVE A BARGAINING CHIP.
MAIKA IS THE GRANDDAUGHTER OF THE QUEEN OF WOLVES. HER AUNT IS THE WARLORD OF THE DAWN COURT. NO MATTER HOW HUMAN SHE LOOKS, SHE IS ONLY TWO GENERATIONS REMOVED FROM THE MOST POWERFUL ANCIENT STILL ALIVE.
THE WITCHES WOULD PAY DEARLY FOR ONE LIKE HER. THEY MIGHT EVEN LET US BE.
I'VE HEARD SCHEMES LIKE THESE BEFORE. THEY NEVER END WELL.

THEN I'LL RANSOM THE HALFWOLF TO HER MOTHER'S PEOPLE.
THE DAWN COURT WOULD TAKE THAT AS AN ACT OF WAR. THE QUEEN OF WOLVES WOULD BECOME PERSONALLY INVOLVED. EVEN IN HER DECLINE SHE IS A MOST TERRIBLE FOE.

NO ANCIENT HAS AS MUCH POWER AS MY OWN RIGHT HAND, SEIZI. THEY'RE DOOMED CREATURES.

ARE THEY? I WONDER.
SEIZI IS RIGHT, MY LOVE. WE CANNOT SELL NOR RANSOM MAIKA HALFWOLF.
BUT WE CAN STILL USE HER.

THE HALFWOLF SAILS TO THE ISLE OF BONES. THERE SHE WILL FIND THE MASTER OF THAT TERRIBLE MADNESS. IF OUR NIECE DOESN'T CATCH UP TO HER FIRST.
DID YOU ACTUALLY MEET HIM, SEIZI?

SO, WE'VE ARRIVED. UBASTI WATCHES OVER THE FOOLISH AND THE BOLD ALIKE.
I WASN'T EXPECTING OTHER SHIPS TO BE HERE.

YOU'RE NOT THE ONLY ONE WHO WANTS TO LAND ON THE ISLE. TREASURE HUNTERS, MIRACLE SEEKERS, THE HOPELESS...YOU MIGHT HAVE SOME COMPANY ONCE YOU HIT LAND.
SIR? PARDON ME, BUT I THINK YOU SHOULD TIGHTEN THAT BOLT. IF THE VIBRATION OF THE ENGINE LOOSENS IT TOO MUCH, THERE MIGHT BE A SPILL OF OIL AND THE PROPELLER WILL BREAK DOWN.

MY... MY MOTHER WAS...IS... A MECHANIC. SHE...SHE ALWAYS SAID ANYONE COULD LEARN THE LANGUAGE OF MACHINES. YOU JUST HAVE TO LISTEN.

I'LL CHECK ON IT BEFORE IT LAUNCHES.
HALFWOLF.

A GULL JUST DELIVERED A ROYAL ORDER FROM THE BLOOD QUEEN HERSELF. ONE OF HER SHIPS IS APPROACHING. YOU'RE TO WAIT HERE UNTIL IT ARRIVES.
NO.

HA.
JAN. IS THAT SKIFF READY?

YOU SHOULDN'T MAKE THIS ATTEMPT WITHOUT ANOTHER HAND, HALFWOLF.

I'M SURE I SHOULD, CAPTAIN. AND SO ARE YOU.

YOU CAN'T TELL THE BLOOD QUEEN I STOLE YOUR SKIFF IF ONE OF YOUR SAILORS IS WITH ME.

MISS! MASTER REN! PLEASE DON'T GO WITHOUT ME!

JUST LOOKING AT THAT MIST MAKES ME RECONSIDER OUR ALLIANCE.

STAY ON THE SHIP THEN. IT MIGHT BE SAFER... AS LONG AS ANOTHER BOMB DOESN'T GO OFF.

A TEMPTING OFFER...

...AND THEN I REMEMBER THAT NOT A SINGLE NEKOMANCER HAS EVER MANAGED TO SET FOOT ON THE ISLE OF BONES.

I'M COMING BECAUSE I LIKE MAKING THE POETS TALK ABOUT ME...

...AND BECAUSE I SUSPECT YOU MIGHT HAVE NEED OF A CAT BEFORE THIS NONSENSE IS THROUGH.

Mother, why did I follow you to this place? Sometimes I do things for you, and later, it is as if I woke from a dream...
KIPPA!
WAIT.

Pleasing you doesn't always seem worth the price of staying alive.
SHE CAN SWIM NOW.

But every time I am near death, I hear your commands...
GASP!

...and I fight.
NNHG!

Because you taught me...

...to fear your disapproval more than I fear death.
ONLY A DOG FOLLOWS SOMEONE SO BLINDLY.
IS THAT WHAT YOU ARE? A DOG?
SNFF
HUFF
HUFF
HUFF

Should I thank you?
SNFF
SNFF
STOP CRYING.
STOP CRYING OR I'LL THROW YOU BACK INTO THE SEA.

Mother Wolf, you called yourself.
I'M SORRY, MISS. BUT I DIDN'T WANT TO BE LEFT BEHIND.
I PROMISE I WON'T SLOW YOU --
What does a wolf teach her pups but teeth and hunger?
You didn't make me in your image.
-- MMPH.
You made me into something worse.

From the archives of the esteemed **Professor Tam Tam**, former First Record-Keeper of the Is'hami Temple, and learned contemporary of Namron Black Claw...

500 DEAD IN KETTARA

THE COUNCIL OF UBASTI DECLARES WAR ON THE FEDERATION

INVASION

In a single night of violence unlike any seen since the time of the Wolf Wars, Federation troops conducted a surprise attack on Ubasti's most Holy City of Kettara, dropping a storm of bombs that ravaged the city and destroyed almost all of its architectural treasures from the First Age. The famed University of Ketta, home to what was a promising new generation of young Poets, is still burning out of control. Most of its student body is feared dead.

"ON THIS DAY, HUMANS STRUCK A DAGGER INTO THE HEARTS OF CATS EVERYWHERE. WE SHALL HAVE OUR REVENGE."

– Nekomancer Thorna Shatterclaw

FEDERATION RESUMES ATTACKS AS CUMAEAN DEFECTORS MEET WITH DUSK COURT

IN A DARING ESCAPE THAT ALMOST ENDED IN CAPTURE, THREE CUMAEAN WITCH-NUNS HAVE BEEN SMUGGLED ACROSS THE WALL BY EDENITE SYMPATHIZERS.

Rumored to be aeronautical engineers from the Cumaean stronghold in Constantine, their presence has already stirred up controversy, from those who fear they are spies, and from others who anticipate the Dusk Court will not share any scientific intelligence with its allied Dawn Court.

CHAPTER TEN

GODDESS, SAVE ME.

HELP ME... PLEASE HELP...

AVENGE US.

MY LOVE... MY LOVE...

WHERE IS MY CHILD?

LOOK AT THEM. THERE MUST BE HUNDREDS... THOUSANDS.

FIND A WAY
I'VE NEVER SEEN SO MANY GHOSTS IN ONE PLACE, NOT EVEN DURING MY MISSION TO THE SITE OF THE KETTARA MASSACRE.
HELP... HELP...
RELEASE ME
SAVE ME
THE STRONGEST NEKOMANCER CAN ONLY HOLD THE DEAD FOR A BRIEF TIME. BUT THESE GHOSTS... ARE OLD. THERE IS POWER HERE.

RUN... FROM... HERE
THE TORMENT...
THEY'RE IN PAIN.
I IMAGINE THEY ARE. IT'S UNNATURAL FOR A SOUL TO BE TRAPPED LIKE THIS.
LEAVE...

SAVE YOURSELVES
SO ALIVE... SO ALIVE...
FEED ME LIFE
ISN'T THIS UNNATURAL, TOO?

DAMN IT!
I'VE NEVER FELT ANYTHING LIKE THIS. WHATEVER HOLDS THEM HERE THRESHES THROUGH THEIR SOULS LIKE A GUTWORM.
MISS?

STAY AWAY FROM US!

MAIKA HALFWOLF!
WHO ARE YOU?
CAPTAIN OF THE BLOOD QUEENS' PERSONAL GUARD.
YOU ARE TO CEASE YOUR JOURNEY TO THE ISLE OF BONES -- IMMEDIATELY.
ARE YOU FUCKING INSANE? YOU NEED TO SWIM OUT OF HERE NOW. THESE WATERS --
WE HAVE ORDERS TO DELIVER YOU TO OUR QUEENS. DO NOT RESIST OR WE WILL HAPPILY KILL YOUR FRIENDS.
JUST AS YOU KILLED OUR SISTER.
LISTEN TO HER! DON'T YOU SEE THE GHOSTS?
WHAT GHOSTS?
I THINK IT'S TOO LATE.

AIIIIIIIIIIIIIIII..!!!

I *TOLD* THEM TO LEAVE.

KIPPA, COME TOWARDS US. SLOWLY.

I'M SCARED.

HHHIIIIIISSSSS...

SEA GHOULS.
"THEY WRAPPED HER CORPSE IN SILVER...
"...A SHROUD IN MOONGLOW MADE...WITH AN ANCIENT'S CHAIN THEY LOWERED HER, WHILE IN PAIN THEIR EYES DID FADE.
"OH, NOW THE STORM IS RAGING, THE SHIP HAS SEEN ITS LAST, AND SHE WILL NEVER SEE THE SUN...AS LONG AS THE BONES STAND STRONG AND FAST."
ANOTHER GHOST IS COMING.
NO. THAT'S SOMETHING WORSE.
NOT WORSE. ONLY THE FERRYMAN.
WHO BEARS THE BONE?

I DO.
I REMEMBER WELL THE ONE WHO BORE IT FROM THIS PLACE. YOU WILL WANT THE SAME THING SHE DID.
THE ISLAND.
GIVE IT TO ME, AND I WILL BEAR YOU THERE.
WE CAN FIND IT OURSELVES.
THEN YOU WILL SAIL UNTIL THE END OF YOUR DAYS. THIS IS MY DOMAIN, MORTAL. NONE MAY SURVIVE IT WITHOUT MY MERCY.
BRING US, THEN.
YOU MUST BE SPECIFIC WHEN NEGOTIATING WITH POWER, HALFWOLF.
WILL YOU GUARANTEE OUR SAFETY, CREATURE? ARE WE UNDER YOUR *PROTECTION?*
YES, ***YES.***
NOW THE ***BONE.***

AH!
ALMOST WHOLE.
GAIN ONE, LOSE ONE.
SNICK
MY PRECIOUS SELF!
THIEF! WRETCHED THIEF! I'LL FLENSE THE FLESH FROM YOUR FACE!
YOU FORGET YOURSELF. WE ARE UNDER YOUR PROTECTION. NOW BRING US TO THE ISLAND. SAFELY.
YOU PLAYED THAT WELL.
MY MOTHER RETURNED WITH A KEY...
...SO I'M GUESSING WE'LL NEED ONE TO LEAVE.

"TO YOU WE CRY, WE SEND UP OUR SIGHS, PLEASE TURN YOUR EYES OF MERCY TOWARD US...
"...BUT I SAY ROW, SISTERS, ROW, THE TIME RUNS FAST, DAYLIGHT IS PAST, YOUR HEAD WILL SPLIT IN THREE...
"I'LL DROP YOU DOWN TO THE BOTTOM OF THE SEA, AND IN THIS EXILE YOU WILL TOIL..."

...THAT IS NO ISLAND... IT IS A GOD... FALLEN WHERE IT STOOD...IN HOLY BATTLE...
...THESE WATERS... ARE THICK... WITH THE PUTRESCENCE... OF ITS DEMISE...
...AND THAT CREATURE... IS MADE OF ITS BONES...
...WHY... WOULD SUCH A DIRE... THING... BE NEEDED...?
MY BODY IS TREMBLING... AS IF MY BONES ARE SUDDENLY DISPLEASED.
I DID NOT KNOW SUCH A THING WAS POSSIBLE.
AND SOMETHING IS DIFFERENT ABOUT YOU, MORTAL.

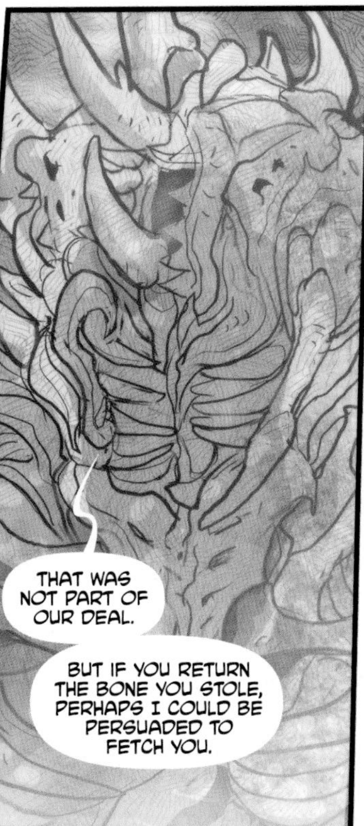

I COULD BE WAITING A LONG TIME, MORTAL!
THE HEART OF THE ISLAND IS A TREACHEROUS PLACE! LEAVE ME THE BONE AND I PROMISE TO WAIT, AND TO DELIVER YOU TO SAFETY!
SO THIS IS WHAT HAPPENS TO THE BODY OF A GOD.
IT GETS SWALLOWED BY THE WORLD.
DO YOU REMEMBER HOW IT DIED? WHAT WEAPON WAS USED?
WERE YOU THERE?
...I...CANNOT... RECALL...
BUT YOU WOULD HAVE KNOWN THIS GOD.
THERE COULDN'T HAVE BEEN THAT MANY OF YOU.
...I REMEMBER.. WEAKNESS..

YOU'RE RUNNING AWAY AGAIN? JUST BECAUSE YOU DON'T WANT TO ANSWER THE QUESTION?
LET ME GUESS... YOU NEED TO TAKE A DEMON NAP.
...NO MORE... SLEEP... FOR ME...

...YOU ARE... ON YOUR QUEST... AND I AM ON... MINE...
...SOMETHING ...IS NOT RIGHT...

...ANY POWER... THAT CAN RENDER...THE BONES OF MY KIND...A PUPPET... IS TO BE TREATED...
...WITH CAUTION...

THE MONSTER SOUNDS SAD, MISS. AND SCARED.
TRY FEELING SYMPATHY FOR IT THE NEXT TIME IT WANTS TO EAT YOU.
I FEEL SYMPATHY FOR YOU... AND YOU TRY TO EAT ME.

...IS THERE NO... END... TO THIS... DARKNESS...?
...HAS EVERYTHING... I WAS... BEEN CONSUMED...?
...I SHOULD JUST... KILL THIS PART OF YOU... AND SEE WHAT HAPPENS.
...WOULD YOUR OTHER... SELF... BE KILLED... TOO?
I... WAS ABLE... TO SEE *YOUR* MEMORIES...
...BUT I CANNOT... SEE MY OWN...
...THERE ARE... VAST HOLES... INSIDE ME...
...TOO MUCH SLEEP... TOO MUCH TIME... AWAY FROM... FLESH...
...YOU AND I... LITTLE ONE... ARE GHOSTS...

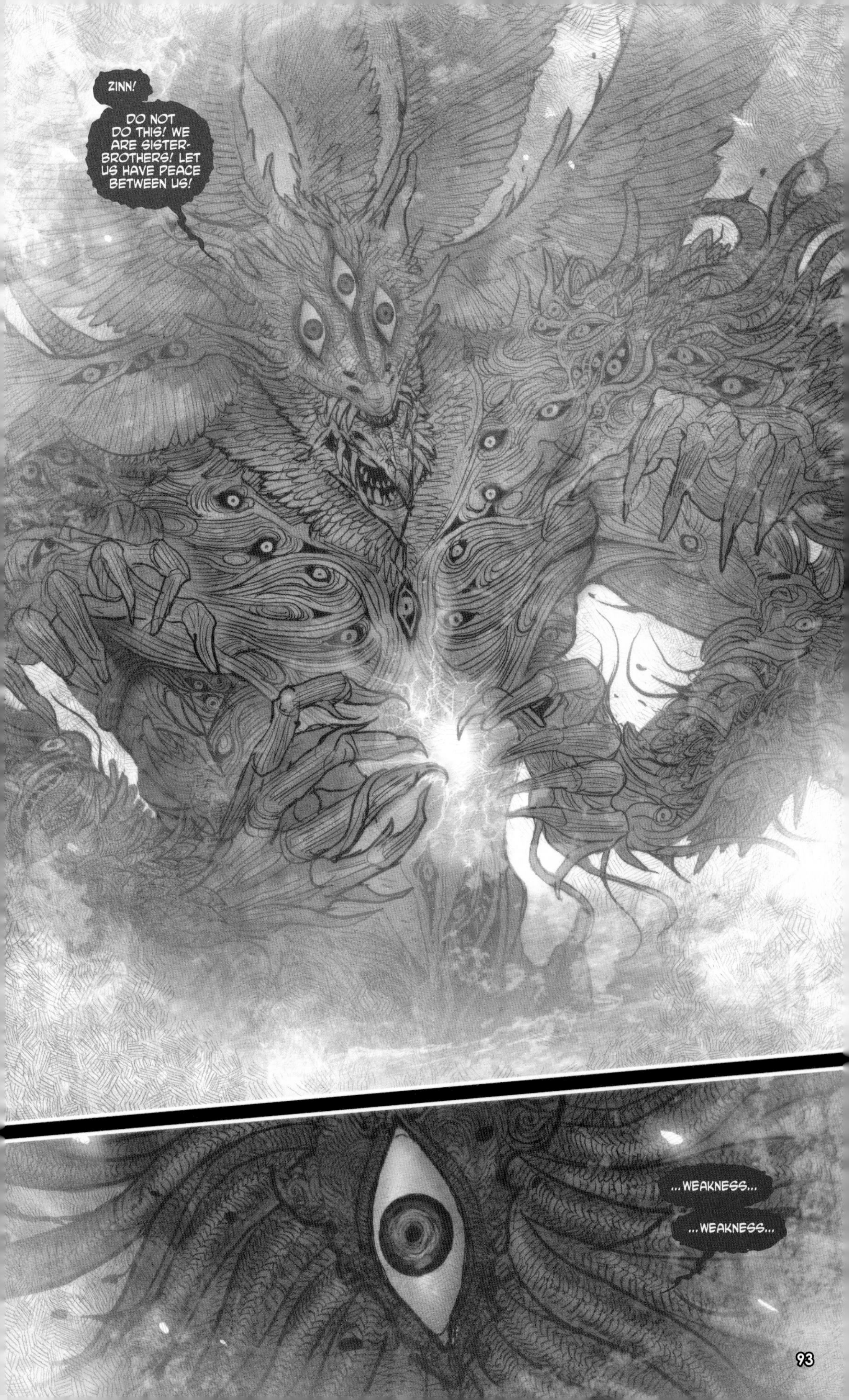
ZINN!
DO NOT DO THIS! WE ARE SISTER-BROTHERS! LET US HAVE PEACE BETWEEN US!
...WEAKNESS...
...WEAKNESS...

YOU'VE BEEN QUIET, CAT.
I THOUGHT YOU'D BE BORING US WITH STORIES ABOUT THIS PLACE, BUT YOU SEEM MORE INTERESTED IN THAT SKULL YOU'RE CARRYING.
THE FERRYMAN APPEARS IN NO RECORDS I AM AWARE OF. ODD, DON'T YOU THINK?
RUN
SEIZI, SYRYSSA, OLD TOOTH -- NONE OF THEM MENTIONED HIM, EITHER... AND THE FERRYMAN CLEARLY REMEMBERED MY MOTHER.
BUT THEY'D HAVE NO REASON TO LIE.
NO. BUT I'M BEGINNING TO FEAR THE STORMFURS, AND EVERYONE ELSE WHO RETURNED FROM THE ISLAND, WERE LESS FORTHCOMING THAN I ASSUMED.
AS SOON AS IT'S NIGHT, I'LL SUMMON THIS SKULL'S GHOST AND GET SOME ANSWERS. THERE'S STILL MEAT ON HIM... HE'LL BE FRESH ENOUGH.
AND THEN THERE'S THE FOX ANCIENT THAT KIPPA DETECTED.
SO WHAT?
WE BOTH KNEW THERE WAS SOMETHING ON THE ISLAND. MY MOTHER DIDN'T COME ALL THIS WAY TO TALK TO A TREE... I DON'T THINK.

BEWARE
RUN
HELP
WE'RE NOT ALONE.
THE STORIES SPEAK OF A WRETCHED POWER THAT LURKS AT THE HEART OF THE ISLAND, CAPABLE OF GREAT GIFTS OR TERRIBLE PUNISHMENT.
BUT UNTIL NOW I DIDN'T KNOW THAT POWER WAS AN ANCIENT. AN EXILE OF THAT MAGNITUDE SHOULD HAVE BEEN RECORDED --
YOU SHOULD HAVE MORE RESPECT FOR YOUR ELDERS, HALFWOLF.
ANCIENTS ARE DIFFICULT TO DEAL WITH UNDER NORMAL CIRCUMSTANCES. NO ANCIENT LIVES IN A PLACE LIKE THIS BECAUSE THEY ARE FULLY SANE.

WELL?
WHERE IS THE FOX?

IN NONE OF THE HISTORIES IS THERE MENTION OF A CITY ON THE ISLE OF BONES. NOTHING OF THIS SCALE OR BEAUTY.

PERHAPS THOSE WHO ESCAPED NEVER LEFT THE BEACH, CAT.

I MIGHT BELIEVE THAT, IF NOT FOR YOUR MOTHER.

THERE ARE SO MANY PEOPLE HERE.

I TOLD YOUR MOTHER SHE WOULD RETURN... FAMISHED, BROKEN, A FAILURE TO HERSELF.
AND SO SHE HAS, THROUGH YOU -- THE RUIN FORETOLD
HOW MAY I BE OF SERVICE, DAUGHTER OF DOOM?

An excerpt of a lecture from the esteemed **Professor Tam Tam**, former First Record-Keeper of the Is'hami Temple, and learned contemporary of Namron Black Claw...
IT IS SAID BY THE POETS THAT IN THE THOUSAND YEARS FOLLOWING THE WAR WITH THE OLD GODS, A DRACUL WAS DISCOVERED HAUNTING THE RIVER AT THE BASE OF THE VALONT HIGHLANDS.
RARE CREATURES, EVEN THEN. BODIES LONG AS A TEMPLE COLUMN, AND JUST AS THICK AROUND; NO ARMS OR LEGS. A PROUD SKULL WITH GOD EYES -- THREE ON EITHER SIDE, BLAZING LIKE SPARKS IN VOLCANIC ASH. DEVOTEES OF FRESH WATER. GODDESS-TOUCHED, SOME WOULD ARGUE -- THOUGH SACRED ORIGINS COULD NOT SAVE THEM.
THE VALONT DRACUL HAD NEVER HARMED ANOTHER, BUT ITS EXISTENCE DROVE SOME ANCIENTS MAD WITH AVARICE. THEY WANTED ITS SKIN, THEY WANTED ITS TEETH, THEY WANTED TO HARVEST ITS BODY AS A TERRIBLE TROPHY AND HANG ITS HEAD SO THAT ALL MIGHT ENVY THEIR MIGHTINESS.
AND YET, THE POETS OF THE AGE DESCRIBE THE FIRST BATTLE BETWEEN THE VALONT DRACUL AND THE ANCIENTS AS A HUMILIATING DEFEAT. THOUGH THEY HAD FOUGHT THE GODS THEMSELVES, THE ANCIENTS WERE UNPREPARED FOR THE MAGNIFICENT POWER OF THE DRACUL.
INSTEAD OF BEING DETERRED, HOWEVER, THIS ONLY MADE THEIR BLOODLUST GROW STRONGER.
THE DRACUL DO NOT KILL...IT WOULD TAINT THEIR SOULS. RATHER THAN FIGHT AGAIN AND RISK BLOODSHED, THE VALONT DRACUL FLED UNDERGROUND THROUGH CAVERNS UNKNOWABLE TO IMMORTALS, DOWN TO A SUNLESS SEA.
IT WAS NEVER SEEN AGAIN. IN TIME, ALL THE DRACULS FLED -- OR WERE HUNTED TO DEATH.
IN ITS HASTE, THE VALONT DRACUL SCRAPED ITS SCALES AGAINST THE STONE WALLS OF THE TUNNELS THROUGH WHICH IT FLED. THOSE SCALES, OVER TIME, GREW INTO THE DAMP ROCK -- FILLING THE DARKNESS WITH A PERMANENT LIGHT THAT, EONS LATER, REFUSES TO BE EXTINGUISHED.
THAT MIGHT HAVE BEEN THE END OF IT...SAVE THAT THESE CAVERNS HAVE SINCE BECOME A SACRED REFUGE TO ALL WHO NEED PROTECTION. IN THE TIME OF THE FIRST EXTERMINATION, ARCANICS VENTURED DEEP INTO THESE CAVES, PRAYING TO THE DRACUL FOR SANCTUARY. WHEN THE CUMAEA CROSSED THE WALL TO INVADE, ARCANICS SENT THEIR CHILDREN TO VALONT, SO THEY MIGHT HIDE IN THE SACRED CAVERNS.
REMEMBER THIS PLACE, KITS. YOU MIGHT HAVE NEED OF A DRACUL'S PROTECTION SOME DAY.
WE ARE ALL, AT TIMES, THE HUNTED.

CHAPTER ELEVEN

ZINN.

HAJIN.
THE OTHERS SEEK YOU.
I COULD NOT STAY. I WAS DISHEARTENED BY THE ARGUMENTS.
I FEAR A GREAT CHANGE IS UPON US.
YES. ONE OF YOUR DESIGN.
NO. SOMETHING DARKER. THE DESTRUCTION OF US, MY FRIEND.
A WAR BETWEEN OUR KIND.

IT WILL NOT COME TO THAT.
EEEEHHH
POOR CREATURE.
THIS IS WHY WE CANNOT STAY HERE.
WE WILL KILL ALL LIFE ON THIS WORLD. EVEN IF WE DO NOT MEAN TO DO SO.
WHERE WILL WE GO? BACK INTO THE SHADOW PLAINS? NOTHING IS THERE FOR US, HAJIN.
WE WERE LOST FOR EONS AND NOW WE ARE NOT. THIS WORLD IS LOVELINESS BEYOND ANYTHING WE EVER DREAMED. YOU CANNOT ASK US TO ABANDON IT.
WE WERE EXILED -- THROWN INTO THE SHADOW PLAINS -- BECAUSE WE WOULD NOT BECOME MURDERERS.
I WILL NOT HAVE US DESTROY OUR PRINCIPLES NOW, AFTER ALL OUR SACRIFICES, OUT OF GREED OR COWARDICE.
THE CREATURES WHO INHABIT THIS WORLD ARE INSIGNIFICANT, UNWORTHY OF OUR BENEFICENCE.
...THAT IS WHAT I TOLD... HAJIN...
...I WAS...A FOOL...

SCHLUUP
YOU'LL HAVE TO FORGIVE ME. YOU ARRIVED AT AN INOPPORTUNE TIME.
WHO ARE THESE PEOPLE? WHAT ARE YOU DOING TO THEM?
YOU CAN FIND FIRE... BURN ME FROM LIFE... END THIS...
ME? I'VE DONE NOTHING. THIS ISLAND HAS A MIND OF ITS OWN... AND THAT MIND IS CRUEL... AND TERRIFYING.
STAY HERE LONG ENOUGH AND YOU WILL BEGIN TO CHANGE. I'VE MADE EVERY EFFORT TO STALL THAT PROCESS FOR THESE POOR SOULS WHO HAVE BEEN STRANDED HERE OVER THE YEARS.
BUT EVEN A DEAD GOD EXERTS POWER.
...WATER... FOR ME... WATER...
...HELP...
...FREE US...
...ASK HIM...
...PLEASE...

SHOW ME THE MARK, DAUGHTER OF DOOM. I KNOW YOU BEAR IT. I CAN FEEL IT GLARING AT ME FROM YOUR SKIN.
MY MOTHER WAS *HERE.* SOMETHING *YOU* SAID TO HER LED TO THIS.
WHAT *AM* I? WHAT IS *INSIDE* ME?
WHAT DOES THIS MEAN TO YOU?
IT MEANS THAT MORIKO SUCCEEDED.
IN MOST OF MY VISIONS, SHE DID NOT. IN MOST... SHE WAS OBLITERATED.
YOU DIDN'T ANSWER MY QUESTION.
MORIKO'S DAUGHTER, OF ALL PEOPLE, SHOULD KNOW THAT NOTHING IS FREE.
I PROVIDED YOUR MOTHER WITH THE INFORMATION SHE CRAVED SO DESPERATELY BECAUSE IN A VISION I SAW MY CHAINS BROKEN... BY YOU.
BREAK THIS CHAIN, AND I WILL TELL YOU WHAT YOU NEED TO KNOW.

BEFORE YOU MAKE ANY DEALS, HALFWOLF, IT'S IMPORTANT TO ASCERTAIN EXACTLY WHO WE'RE DEALING WITH.
EXALTED ONE, ARE YOU LORD ROHAR THE INSATIABLE... KNOWN DEMOTICALLY AS... THE BLOOD FOX?
AM I? NO ONE HAS CALLED ME THAT IN A THOUSAND YEARS... AND I HAVE BEEN TRAPPED IN THIS CURSED PRISON TWICE THAT LONG.
A PRISON, IS IT? MORE LIKE A HELL.
THERE IS A PRICE FOR AUDACITY.
SAVE... MY... CHILD...
WHAT THE CAT WOULD INFORM YOU, WERE I NOT HERE TO CHECK HIS TONGUE, IS THAT IN MANY EPOCHS PAST I LED A POGROM AGAINST YOUR HALF-BREED ANCESTORS...
FOR REASONS WE COULD NOT EXPLAIN, WHEN YOUR KIND FIRST APPEARED OUR POWER BEGAN TO DECLINE... IT SEEMED YOU HALFBREEDS WERE DRAINING OUR MAGIC.
I TRIED TO REVERSE OUR LOSSES BY KILLING YOU ALL. I NEARLY SUCCEEDED.
YOU... CHILD. YOU ARE PARTIALLY FOX. HOW FAR REMOVED FROM THE PURE, I WONDER?
I... D-DON'T KNOW, SIR. MY MOTHER WAS NOT AS FOX AS ME. BUT MY FATHER ALSO HAD FOX BLOOD. THERE WERE LOTS OF US IN THE NORTH.
ONE CAN BE SURE OF THAT. YOUR KIND BREED VERY FAST.
ONCE, YOUR VERY APPEARANCE WOULD HAVE SPELLED YOUR DEATH, CHILD OR NOT.
BUT I HAVE LEFT THAT HATE BEHIND. THE BLOOD FOX IS NO MORE.

THE CHAIN IS WHAT KEEPS YOU HERE?
GIVE ME THE INFORMATION FIRST...OR YOU CAN KEEP ROTTING IN THIS PLACE.
FOR TWO THOUSAND YEARS I'VE LANGUISHED IN THIS CARCEL. I CAN WAIT, CHILD. BUT YOU, I SUSPECT, CANNOT.
THE FOX BLUFFS. HE DOESN'T KNOW SHIT.
LET'S GO.
DO NOT BE SO IMPULSIVE, HALFWOLF...
MAIKA.
PLEASE DO AS HE ASKS.

FUCK YOU.

MY MOTHER NEVER SAID *PLEASE.*

VERY WELL...
...I WILL PROVIDE YOU WITH THE INFORMATION.

BUT SWEAR AN OATH ON YOUR SACRED BLOOD THAT YOU WILL BREAK MY CHAINS!

I SWEAR. ON MY MOTHER.

BEFORE WE BEGIN, SHOW ME THE MASK. I KNOW YOU HAVE IT.
WHAT GHASTLY BEAUTY.
WHAT DO YOU KNOW ABOUT THE OLD GODS?
I USED TO THINK THEY WERE DEAD... THAT WHAT WE SEE IN THE SKY ARE THEIR GHOSTS. I DON'T BELIEVE THAT ANYMORE.
WE ANCIENTS REMEMBER WHEN THE OLD GODS FIRST FOUND THIS WORLD... AND TRIED TO DESTROY IT.
THE LONG WAR THAT LED TO THEIR IMPRISONMENT... LET US JUST SAY THAT FEW OF US ELDERS WILL EVER FORGET IT. THE SCARS ARE TOO DEEP...

THE ONE YOU NOW CALL THE SHAMAN-EMPRESS DID NOT LIVE THROUGH THOSE DARK TIMES. PERHAPS IF SHE HAD SHE WOULD NOT HAVE BEEN SO FOOLISH...
UNDERSTAND: EVEN BEFORE HER ASCENSION, SHE WAS VERY POWERFUL. HER MIND WAS UNLIKE ANY THAT CAME BEFORE -- PROFOUND AND FAR-SEEING, BUT EVER RESTLESS.
IT WAS PERHAPS INEVITABLE THAT SHE WOULD BE DRAWN TO THE OLD GODS. PERHAPS IT WAS A MATTER OF AMBITION. PERHAPS THEY CALLED HER TO THEM. WHO CAN SAY?

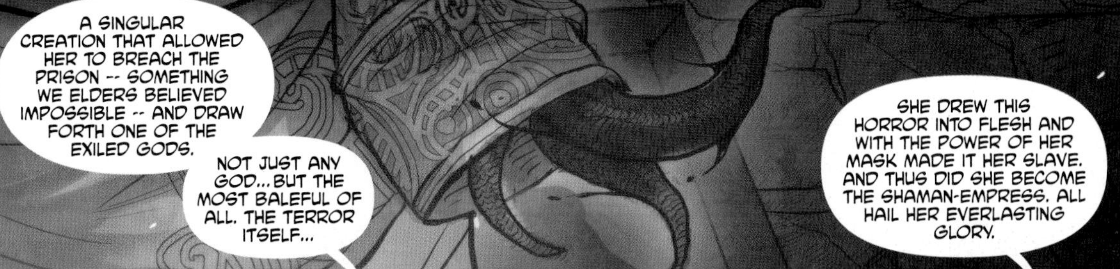

LONG THE LADY AND HER MONSTER REIGNED. BUT NOTHING IS TRULY EVERLASTING. IT WAS SAID THAT THE VERY MONSTER WHICH HAD ELEVATED HER... SLOWLY DEVOURED HER.

PERHAPS THAT SOUNDS FAMILIAR.

WHY DID YOU LEAVE? DON'T YOU WANT TO LEARN MORE ABOUT MISS?

TO QUOTE THE POETS... IT IS POSSIBLE TO DROWN IN INFORMATION... AND DIE FOR LACK OF WISDOM.

IT WOULD BE UNWISE FOR US TO BE DISTRACTED BY THE TALES OF THE BLOOD FOX, HOWEVER TRUE THEY MIGHT BE.

HOW DID YOU KNOW HIS NAME?

PERHAPS ≈SNIFF≈ YOU WOULD LIKE TO... EAT... BEFORE HEARING MORE?
YOU LOOK... A TAD... PECKISH. THE SHAMAN-EMPRESS WAS THE SAME.
HER... APPETITES... WERE LEGION. IT WAS UNWISE TO REASON WITH HER WHEN SHE WAS... HUNGRY.

I'M FINE.
HEH.

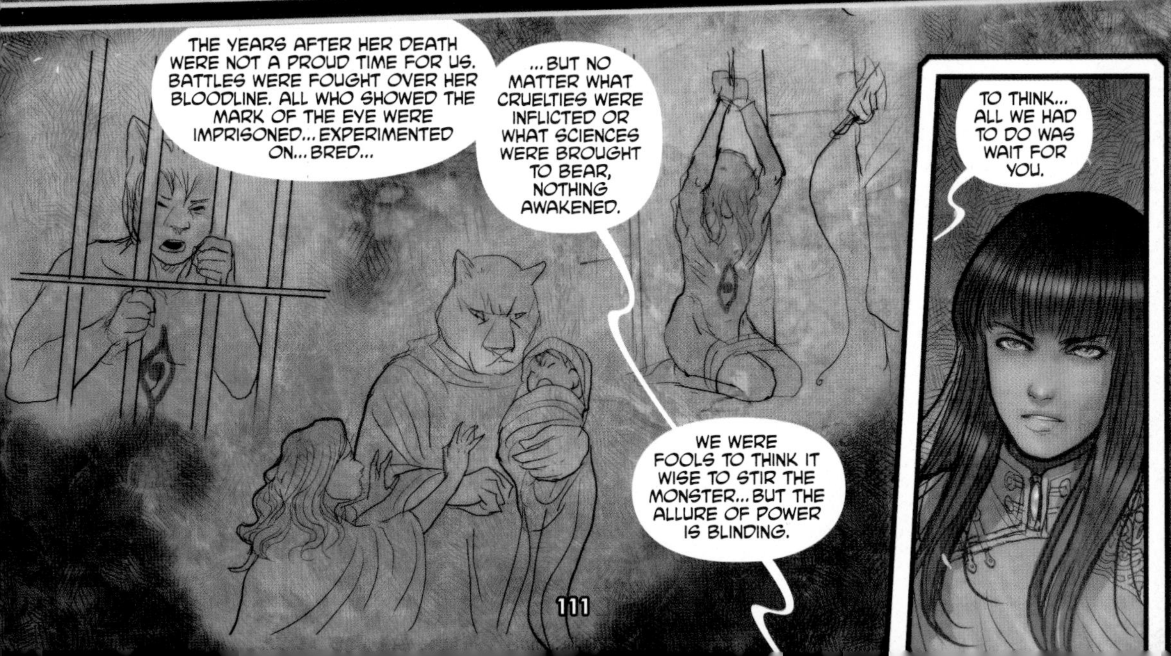

THEN I... I WAS JUST...

A GAMBLE. AN EXPERIMENT.

YOUR MOTHER WANTED WHAT ALL THE OTHERS HAVE DESIRED. CONTROL OVER THE BLOOD.

AND MORIKO DID WHAT ALL MOTHERS DO WHEN THEY WANT CONTROL -- SHE HAD A DAUGHTER.

I DON'T WANT THIS POWER.

WHAT I WANT, FOX, IS FOR YOU TO TELL ME HOW TO GET RID OF IT.

THERE'S NO POWER LEFT IN THE WORLD THAT COULD DO WHAT YOU ASK, SAVE THE MASK. ASSEMBLE IT, THEN PERHAPS...
...BUT THAT FUTURE IS DARK TO ME. I DO NOT SEE ITS POSSIBILITY.
I'LL TAKE EVEN THE SMALLEST CHANCE. I DON'T WANT TO BE A MONSTER.
BEFORE HER DEATH THE SHAMAN-EMPRESS PROPHESIZED THAT AT THE END OF TIME HER BLOOD WOULD RISE AGAIN.
SHE SPOKE OF A FINAL WAR -- MORE TERRIBLE THAN ANY THIS WORLD HAD EVER SEEN -- AND THAT IT WOULD BE HER BLOOD THAT WOULD DECIDE THE FATE OF ALL OUR RACES.
YOUR BLOOD.
YOU STAND AT THE CENTER OF THIS PROPHECY. YOU ARE THE SHAMAN-EMPRESS'S DOOM...
...BUT YOU DON'T DESERVE THAT POWER. NO MORE THAN SHE DID. THE FATE OF MY GREAT RACE SHOULD NOT BE IN THE HANDS OF THE DEFILED. OF MONGRELS.

IT IS TIME FOR YOU TO BREAK MY CHAINS.
YOU SWORE AN OATH.
THAT'S ALL YOU HAVE? YOU'VE GIVEN ME NOTHING I CAN USE!
YOU KILLED HOW MANY OF MY KIND IN YOUR DAY? I'M GUESSING YOU'D BE HAPPY TO KILL SOME MORE.
I'M NOT BREAKING SHIT. IF YOU CAN SEE THE FUCKING FUTURE, YOU SHOULD HAVE SEEN THIS COMING.
I DID.
AH!
SHHUNK!

HA! AFTER ALL THESE YEARS!
I KNEW YOU WERE AWAKE INSIDE HER! HOW MUST IT FEEL TO BE TIED TO SOMEONE OTHER THAN YOUR EMPRESS?
...STINKING DOTARD...I REMEMBER YOU...
SHALL I GET ON MY KNEES AND PRAY?!
...YOU DEMANDED... THE EXECUTION... OF MY EMPRESS...
YOU SHOULD HAVE KILLED ME THEN!
...YES... BUT THAT WAS NOT... HER WAY...
...AND I WAS NOT... HER WEAPON... OR HER SLAVE...
AAAAHHHH!!
DAMN YOU!
FOR ONCE... I COMMEND YOU...
I -- NNGH -- STILL HAD MORE QUESTIONS.
I'M SURPRISED YOU DIDN'T TRY TO EAT HIM.
...HE REEKS...OF POISON...
WE MUST HURRY.
KOFF

...SO HUNGRY...
...FORGIVE US...
...WE MUST EAT...
WHY ARE YOU DOING THIS?

...HE SAID WE COULD HAVE YOU...
...BUT NOT THE GIRL-WEAPON...
...HER PARTS... WILL BE HARVESTED... LATER...
I AM... *NNGH*... NOT... GOING TO DIE... AS ANYONE'S... MEAL...

WHA --
HNNN?
SLASH
AAAGH!
CHOMP
NNNNGGGH
WHAT DID YOU DO TO THEM, MASTER REN?
I SUSPECT IT'S BETTER TO ASK WHAT THE HALFWOLF MIGHT HAVE DONE TO THE BLOOD FOX.
FMP
FUMP

WHAT'S HAPPENING TO THIS VILLAGE?
IT WAS NOTHING BUT AN ILLUSION THE FOX LORD CREATED... AND NOW IT IS SLIPPING FROM HIS CONTROL.
JUST AS ALL THE PEOPLE TRAPPED HERE ARE FINALLY FREE OF HIS GLAMOUR. EVEN IF THERE'S LITTLE ENOUGH LEFT OF THEIR MINDS TO APPRECIATE IT.
EEP!
WHY ARE YOU DIFFERENT?
CRASHH
RUUMMMB
I WAS STRANDED HERE SEVEN YEARS AGO DURING A RECONNAISSANCE. THE FOX HAD NEVER MET A CUMAEA. MY... SLIGHT RESISTANCE... TO HIS GLAMOUR INTRIGUED HIM.
SO I LIVED.
TELL ME, DEMON CHILD... WHO WON THE WAR?
CRASHH
RUUMMMBLE
WE DESTROYED EVERY LAST ONE OF YOU FUCKING WITCHES. ARCANICS OCCUPY THE FEDERATION OF MAN AND EVERY HUMAN WHO WORE THE UNIFORM NOW LIVES IN THE SAME SLAVE CAMPS YOU KEPT US IN DURING THE WAR.
AH. I KNEW IT WAS NEVER GOING TO END WELL.
HURRY. THE BEACH IS JUST BEYOND THE MINE.

...NOT EVEN... OUR MOST TERRIBLE ENEMIES... DEFILED OUR CORPSES...
...THERE WAS... HONOR...
LIKE YOU SHOULD TALK. THERE'S NEVER HONOR WHERE THERE'S POWER.
...NO... IT IS NOT... POSSIBLE...
...THERE IS STILL A HUM... IN THESE BONES... A VOICE... THAT IS FAMILIAR...
...SPEAK... TO ME...
WHAT... WHERE HAVE YOU TAKEN US?
MY... CURSED... MEMORIES...
...THIS WORLD IS OURS, HAJIN...
...WE CANNOT SUCCUMB TO THE WEAKNESS THAT LED TO OUR FIRST EXILE. WE MUST BE STRONG ENOUGH TO MAKE THE HARD CHOICES.
...ONCE AND FOR ALL I WILL NOT PERMIT YOU TO SEND US INTO EXILE FOR THESE MORTALS...

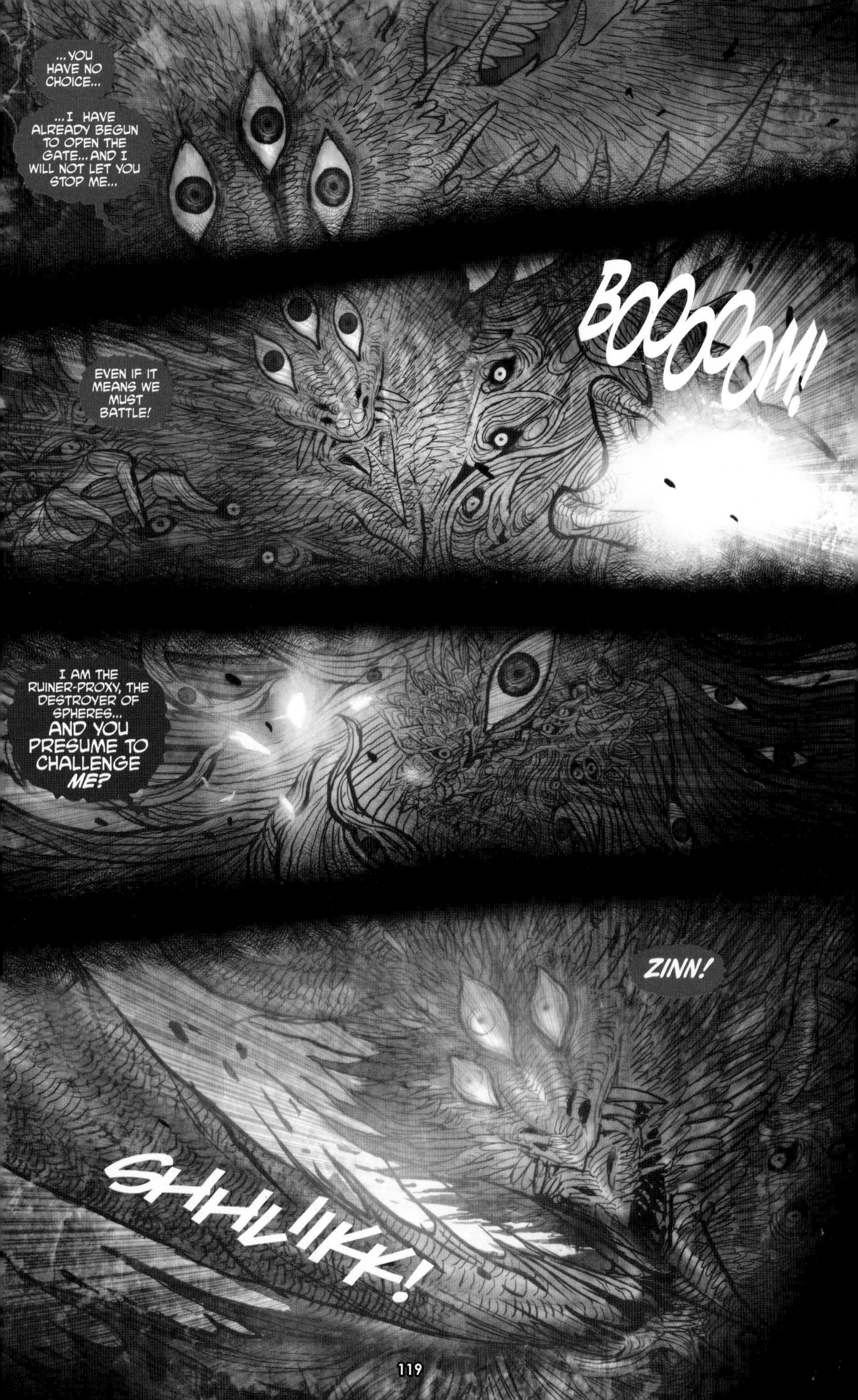
...YOU HAVE NO CHOICE...
...I HAVE ALREADY BEGUN TO OPEN THE GATE... AND I WILL NOT LET YOU STOP ME...
EVEN IF IT MEANS WE MUST BATTLE!
BOOOOOM!
I AM THE RUINER-PROXY, THE DESTROYER OF SPHERES... AND YOU PRESUME TO CHALLENGE ME?
ZINN!
SHHLIKK!

...YOU... BETRAYER... YOU... WHO COULD NOT TOLERATE... MERCY FOR THOSE LESS POWERFUL THAN YOU...
...YOU WILL NEVER... BE REDEEMED...
AAAH!
...NO... NO... THESE BONES... BELONG TO MY... SISTER-BROTHER...
THIS IS NO TIME FOR SOME BLASTED DEMONIC SEIZURE.
YOU -- *KOFF* -- KILLED THAT GOD...
...NO... WE WERE... FRIENDS...
...HOW... COULD... I...
BECAUSE YOU ARE A MONSTER.

YOU LED THE CHARGE THAT WOULD HAVE DESTROYED MY KIND.
AND HERE YOU ARE, WEAK AND ALONE.
YOU ARE MINE NOW. BOTH OF YOU.

DEGRADATION
INSANITY
A FLOWER FROM THE DEMONIC GARDEN
DREAMTAR
A VICIOUS VICE CORRUPTING OUR YOUTH!
IMMORALITY
ONE MOMENT OF BLISS
A LIFETIME OF REG

An excerpt of a lecture from the esteemed **Professor Tam Tam**, former First Record-Keeper of the Is'hami Temple, and learned contemporary of Namron Black Claw...

The years immediately following the Great War were difficult ones for the Arcanic Realms. Whole families, entire bloodlines, had been wiped out, countless communities ravaged, a generation of youth enslaved by the Cumaea and the Federation of Man – or fallen in the desperate fight for freedom. Not a single Arcanic across the known lands, from Dusk to Dawn Court, could say they had not lost friends or family in the Great War.

It was a collective wound – and like many wounds, this one festered. In the aftermath of the war, Arcanics were left disillusioned, disoriented, traumatized. And into this desolation, came dreamtar.

A powerful narcotic derived from the mature blossom of the popei flower, dreamtar is viciously addictive to non-cats. Few who smoke it escape the extract's terrible grasp. In what became an all too familiar irony, many of the same Arcanics who survived the horrors of the war succumbed to the ravages of addiction.

Cats who long cultivated the popei flower for its aromatic qualities are often accused of introducing dreamtar to Arcanic populations. Never speak of the flower or carry it or its essence on your person in non-cat lands. Many a cat has been lynched for carrying as little as a petal in their pouch...

CHAPTER TWELVE

I CAN SMELL THE SHAMAN-EMPRESS BENEATH YOUR SKIN. THREE THOUSAND YEARS AND I HAVE NEVER FORGOTTEN THAT STENCH.
SHE MADE THIS CHAIN THAT BINDS ME, CREATED THIS BLASTED PRISON...BECAUSE SHE KNEW... SHE KNEW...ONE DAY IT WOULD BE NEEDED.
THAT INFERNAL WITCH TOOK HER REVENGE FROM THE GRAVE...

...FOOL...
...THE FOX...IS PLAYING...WITH YOUR MIND...
...YOU ARE...WHOLE... YOU HAVE NOT YET...BEEN DAMAGED...
FIVE YEARS AGO, I FELT YOUR BLOOD AWAKEN. THE WHOLE WORLD FELT IT.
...AND THIS ISLAND SHOOK AND THE BONES CRACKED OPEN...
...DO NOT SUCCUMB... TO ILLUSIONS... YOU WRETCHED... CHILD --
...IN THE AFTERMATH, I DISCOVERED THE SECRET OF THE GODS.
AAH!
SSLLSHH
MY... FLESH...!
NOT ONLY ARE YOU INFERNAL DEMONS MORTAL...
...YOU'RE USEFUL WHEN YOU'RE DEAD.
GET OUT... OF MY FUCKING... MIND...
NNNGH! WHY ARE YOU RUNNING? I THOUGHT IT WAS ALL AN ILLUSION!
...MY BLOOD... IS... REAL...
...THE FOX... HAS COVERED... HIS CLAWS... IN THE BONES... OF MY KIND...
...AND...I AM... VULNERABLE...

GODDESS, GET THE MONSTER OUT OF ME! GET HER OUT!
MAIKA... YOU KNOW WHAT YOU ARE...
...YOU KNOW WHO REALLY KILLED HER...
GASP
YOU SHOULD HAVE GIVEN ME SHARPER TEETH, YOU FUCKING ASSHOLE.
YOU'RE HIDING AGAIN. ONE SCRATCH AND YOU FALTER. SOME DEMON YOU ARE.
...I HAVE NEVER...KNOWN... THE COLOR...OF MY BLOOD...BUT IT...IS FITTING...
...I HAVE BEEN DELIVERED...TO THE SITE...OF MY TRANSGRESSION...
...HOW CAN I NOT...PAY...IN FLESH...AND PAIN...?
WHAT --

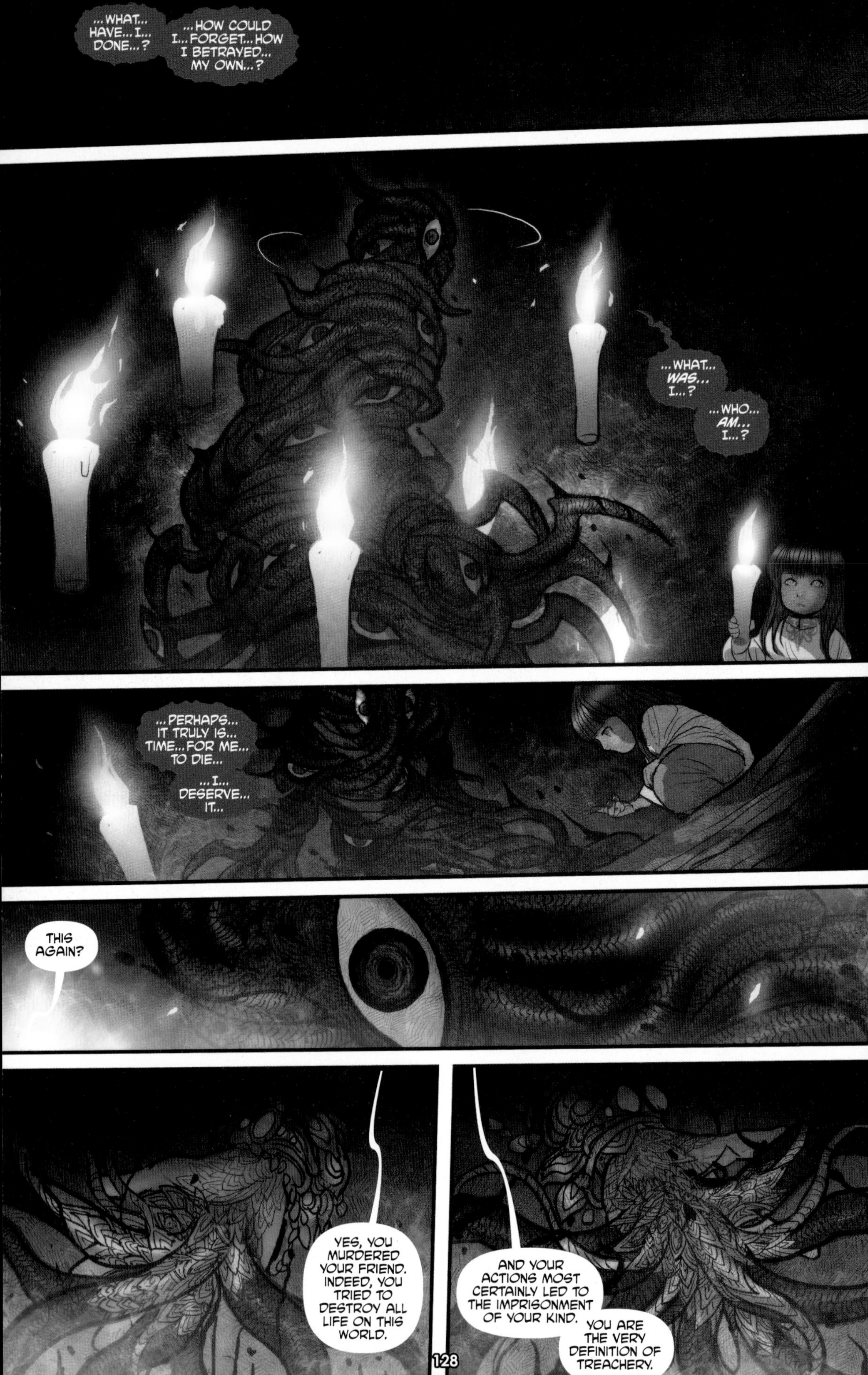
...WHAT... HAVE... I... DONE...?
...HOW COULD I...FORGET...HOW I BETRAYED... MY OWN...?
...WHAT... *WAS*... I...?
...WHO... *AM*... I...?
...PERHAPS... IT TRULY IS... TIME...FOR ME... TO DIE...
...I... DESERVE... IT...
THIS AGAIN?
YES, YOU MURDERED YOUR FRIEND. INDEED, YOU TRIED TO DESTROY ALL LIFE ON THIS WORLD.
AND YOUR ACTIONS MOST CERTAINLY LED TO THE IMPRISONMENT OF YOUR KIND.
YOU ARE THE VERY DEFINITION OF TREACHERY.

BUT GUILT IS SUCH A BORE, MY *QUERIDO.*
YOU WILL NEVER REDEEM YOURSELF.
BUT FOCUS ALWAYS ON YOUR SHAME, AND YOUR SHAME WILL EAT YOU. IT WILL BECOME YOU.
THAT IS THE COWARD'S WAY.
A COWARD NEVER HAS TO LEARN.
BELOVED...

...ZINN... LISTEN TO ME...
THE PAST IS NEVER DEAD. BUT THAT IS WHY IT IS SO PERILOUS. AND USEFUL.
THUMP THUMP
...YOUR ARROGANCE WILL LEAD ONLY TO SUFFERING... AND WAR...
CRSSSSH
WE DO NOT KNOW HOW LONG YOU WILL LIVE BEYOND MY DEATH... BUT SHOULD YOU SURVIVE ME...
...YOU KNOW WHAT TO DO.
...YOU MUST WAKE UP... YOU MUST OPEN YOUR MIND...
DO NOT STOP. DO NOT STOP BECOMING SOMEONE NEW, JUST BECAUSE I AM GONE.
MOVE FORWARD *ALWAYS*... NEVER BACK.
FOR FIVE HUNDRED YEARS I LIVED IN YOUR DARKNESS...
...UNTIL YOU BECAME MY LIGHT...
...DO NOT... LEAVE ME... AGAIN...
...FIND A WAY...

...YOU ASK...
...TOO MUCH...
...OF ME...
...WHAT I AM...
...CANNOT TRULY... CHANGE...
NNNGH!
...OH GODDESS...
WHAT ARE YOU FUCKING MUMBLING ABOUT?
AND WHY DO YOU LOOK LIKE THIS?
BECAUSE THE MONSTER WISHES TO CAST THE GREATEST ILLUSION OF ALL.
THAT IT IS ONE OF US.
BOOM!
DID IT AMUSE YOU, ALL THOSE YEARS AGO? TAKING OUR FORM, MOCKING US WITH YOUR PRESENCE AS YOU WALKED IN THE LIGHT AT THE SIDE OF YOUR MISTRESS?
OR DID YOU FEEL THE WEIGHT OF THE TERRIBLE LEASH THAT BOUND YOU TO MORTAL FLESH? EVEN AS YOU ARE BOUND NOW TO THIS REPULSIVE MONGREL?

...THIS IS... NO...LEASH...
...IT IS...A PROMISE...
...AND YOU... ARE NOT STRONG... ENOUGH...TO BEAR WITNESS...TO THE FULL POWER...OF THAT...VOW...
BUT COME TRY US.
YOU AWFUL CREATURE. I HAVE NO DESIRE TO TAKE YOUR POWER.
WE SHOULD NEVER HAVE TRIED TO HARNESS THE BLOOD. WE SHOULD HAVE ELIMINATED IT ENTIRE --

SSHHRRRIIP
GASP
...EEEAAAGH...
...YOU...ARE... POISON...
...YOU ARE FILLED... WITH THE ESSENCE... OF THE CORPSE... YOU DEFILED...
HEH. MY FLESH DOES NOT PLEASE YOU?
...AND NOW I... AM DEFILED... FROM TASTING... THE FLESH... OF MY SISTER-BROTHER...
...WHY DOES DEFILEMENT... FEEL LIKE... MY SKIN IS ON FIRE...?
IT IS FITTING YOU CHOKE ON YOUR OWN... CONSIDERING YOUR KIND CONSUMED MY BROTHERS AND SISTERS IN THE WAR...
...BUT HOW CURIOUS THAT YOUR MONGREL HOST APPEARS TO SHARE YOUR NEW WEAKNESS...
YOU ARE A POOR INCARNATION OF THE SHAMAN-EMPRESS.
YOU'RE THE ONE IN CHAINS, FATHERFUCKER.
SSHRRIIP
AHHH!
AHHH!
YOU ARE AN OATHBREAKER, JUST LIKE YOUR MOTHER. IF YOU WILL NOT FREE ME FROM THIS CHAIN...
...PERHAPS I WILL BE ABLE TO BREAK IT MYSELF... IF I CONSUME THE FLESH OF THE MONSTER INSIDE YOU...
I'M CLOSE! I'M -- MMPH -- SO VERY CLOSE TO HAVING -- MMMPH -- THE STRENGTH!
CCRRNNCH
...NO...

Mother.
Was it worth it for you?
DAMN IT! WHERE IS HE?!
BEHIND... BE...HIND...
Was I everything you desired?
Or was I just a piece in a greater game?
NNGH!
I'M COMING, MISS!
I CAN SMELL HIM!
GET AWAY FROM THEM!
HEH.
CLEVER CREATURE.

It matters.
CLEVER, BUT ANNOYING.
WHUMP
EEP!
NNGH!
YOU FIRST.
You're gone.
DIE.
And I'm here. Paying the price for your choices.
...I...CAN TELL YOU...WHERE THE REST...OF THE MASK...IS...
...AND THE NAME... OF YOUR... FATHER...
I will never stop paying.
SNAP
GLRG
YOU'VE TOLD ME ENOUGH.
I WAS WRONG TO COME HERE.
...MAY THE BELOVED...CHASE YOUR SOUL...INTO THE ABYSS...

HHSSSSSSS
WHAM
MISS!
DEMON, STAND, OR GET BACK INTO MY BODY. WE NEED TO MOVE, NOW.
WE MUST BE CERTAIN...
YES. HE'S TRULY DEAD.
THE OTHER ANCIENTS WILL HAVE FELT HIS PASSING.
GOOD. FUCK THEM ALL.
LICK LICK
YOU BROKE THE FIRST SEAL! SNAPPED THE BONES. *MY PRISONER IS DEAD.*
WHAT HAVE YOU DONE?!
WHAT HAVE YOU DONE?!
"COME ALL YE YOUNG WOMEN TO THE BONE BEACH GRAVE OH HAIL, OH HAIL... ALL WHO CRAVE THE BLADE YE MUST PAY, YE MUST PAY..."
REMEMBER YOUR PROMISE, FERRYMAN!
MAKE ONE MISTAKE, MORTAL, AND I WILL SPEAR YOUR SOUL UPON THE PROW OF MY SHIP.

WAIT!
MISS, WHAT ARE WE GOING TO DO? THERE ARE SO MANY OF THEM.
TOO MANY FOR THIS BOAT.
WE CAN... NNGH... TAKE A FEW...
DON'T LEAVE US!
HELP!
CHOMP
CHOMP
CHOMP
SPARE THEM. YOUR PRISONER IS GONE. YOU DON'T NEED MORE LIVES.
INGRATE. I GUARD MORE THAN HIM.
THIS ISLAND... THESE BONES... THAT IS MY TRUE CHARGE. THAT IS WHY I EXIST.
NONE SHALL ESCAPE ME.
AND THOSE WHO DO... MUST STILL PAY A PRICE.

CAT... IF THE FERRYMAN DIES, WILL THE GHOSTS BE FREED?
HALFWOLF... DON'T EVEN THINK ABOUT IT. WE ALREADY FOUGHT ONE WAR OVER THE BODIES OF ARCANICS.
IMAGINE IF OTHERS DISCOVER THE POWER THAT COULD BE GAINED FROM HARVESTING THE BONES OF A DEAD GOD.
THE PEOPLE ON THAT ISLAND WERE TORTURED BY THE BLOOD FOX. NO ONE WILL BE ABLE TO RESCUE THEM.
AND THESE SOULS... THEY'RE SLAVES.
SLAVES?
NO... THEY ARE MY *SWEETS.*
FUCK.
MISS. IF YOU WANT TO... TRY TO SAVE THEM... I'LL HELP.
YOU... DEMON. TIME TO FIGHT.
...FIGHT...?
...WE ARE... *DYING...*
NO! YOU CAN'T DIE.
...I ACCEPT... YOUR SACRIFICE... LITTLE ONE... COME CLOSER...
"WHISTLE AND SING YE DAUGHTERS WITH WINGS FOLLOW THE MOON PLUNGE FATHOMS DEEP..."
LEAVE HER ALONE.

THIS ISN'T OVER. ONE DAY I'LL END YOU.
ONLY MY CREATOR CAN UNDO ME, HALFWIT. BUT PLEASE DO RETURN. I WOULD DEARLY LOVE TO SUP ON YOUR SOUL.
OH, NO... NO. NO. NO...
MASTER REN?
WHAT IS IT, CAT?
TELL ME... THERE WAS A CITY ON THAT ISLAND, WASN'T THERE? WHAT DID IT LOOK LIKE?
I... I THINK THERE WAS. BUT IT'S ALL... FUZZY...
MAIKA HALFWOLF!
IS THAT YOU?
THANK GODDESS THE MISTS ARE LIFTING!
LADY HALFWOLF. I'M PLEASED TO FIND YOU LOOKING MOSTLY ALIVE. WE FEARED THE WORST.
I AM CAPTAIN ELISANDRA, AT YOUR SERVICE. MY AUNTS, THE BLOOD QUEENS, HAVE REQUESTED YOUR PRESENCE AT THE CITADEL.
FORGIVE ME IF I DON'T GIVE A FUCK.
FORGIVEN.

WE WERE ALL TAKING BETS YOU WOULDN'T RETURN. GLAD YOU DID.
WHAT DID YOU SEE?
...I'M NOT... SURE. ALL I REMEMBER CLEARLY IS THE BEACH.
WHAT DO YOU THINK THE BLOOD QUEENS WANT WITH MISS?
I REMEMBER YOU AS A CHILD. YOU AND MY COUSIN WERE DEAR FRIENDS.
YOU PLAYED ROUGH.
NOT MUCH HAS CHANGED.
ONE THING HAS.
AREKA NEVER RETURNED FROM YOU AND YOUR MOTHER'S... EXPEDITION.
AREKA...?
THE PHOTO...
...WE WILL NOT... SURVIVE... THIS POISON... UNLESS WE --
I KNOW WHAT YOU WANT AND THE ANSWER IS NO.
...YOU ARE...EVER PREDICTABLE...
AHHH!
...BUT WE... DO NOT HAVE... TIME...FOR DEBATE...
SLLICE

AHHH!
AGHH!!
ARRGH!!
AIIEEE!
OH, MISS.
YOU KILLED THEM ALL. EVERY LAST ONE.
...NO...IT IS WE...IT IS US...WHO FED...
DOESN'T IT MATTER TO YOU? IS EVERY LIFE BUT YOURS SO FUCKING WORTHLESS?
...SURVIVAL... IS NOT... GENTLE...
...MERCY... IS FOR THE... WEAK...
IS THAT WHY YOU MURDERED YOUR FRIEND?
IS THAT WHAT YOU WHISPERED TO THE SHAMAN-EMPRESS?
YOU SAID YOU WEREN'T HER SLAVE...BUT MAYBE SHE WAS YOURS. HOW LONG DID IT TAKE YOU TO TURN HER INTO A MURDERER?

"THE HALFWOLF KILLED THEM ALL, DIDN'T SHE? AND A MEMBER OF THE BLOOD QUEEN'S OWN."

I'M GOING TO THROW HER OVERBOARD.

CAPTAIN... ALL DUE RESPECT, BUT WE HAVE ORDERS FROM COMMANDER IMURA.

THINK OF YOUR OATH.

"WHAT GOOD ARE OATHS IF SHE MURDERS US ALL?

"I WILL NOT TAKE THE RISK.

GASP
IT'S YOUR FAULT, YOU KNOW. YOU COULD HAVE JUST COME HOME WHEN YOU WERE SUMMONED INSTEAD OF BEING HUNTED LIKE AN ANIMAL.

IT'S TIME, LADY HALFWOLF, TO FACE THE CHARGES AGAINST YOU. UNLESS YOU HAVE THE WEAPON...OR KNOW WHERE IT IS.

IN THAT CASE, THE WARLORD WILL SURELY FORGIVE YOU FOR THE MURDERS YOU COMMITTED.

YOU SHOULD NEVER HAVE COME HERE.

YOU SHOULD HAVE *LIED* TO MY SISTER AND TOLD HER I WAS DEAD.

AND WHY WOULD WE DO THAT?

LITTLE WOLF.

YOUR TEETH.

AIIIIGGGGH!

CRUNCH

SLLIISSSHH

WHAT... WHAT ARE YOU...?
...YOU'RE TOO STRONG...
SLLASHH
MY SISTER WILL NEVER HAVE MY SECRETS.
SLLASHH
SHE'S TOO WEAK TO HOLD THEM.
SLLASHH
THE REST ARE DEAD. WE ARE FORTUNATE YOUR SISTER DID NOT SEND A LARGER SQUAD.
HERE. I FOUND THIS ON ONE OF THEM.
AIIEE!
WHEN THE WARLORD -- *PANT* -- FINDS OUT -- *PANT* -- YOU HAVE A DAUGHTER --
WHO WILL TELL HER?
MRPH!

I'M SORRY I DIDN'T DO MORE, MOTHER.
I WAS SCARED.
SO WAS I. I WAS AFRAID THEY WOULD TAKE YOU FROM ME.
BOOM
WHY WOULD THEY DO THAT?
TO HURT ME.
AND, EVENTUALLY, TO HURT *YOU.* TO TRY AND MAKE YOU INTO SOMETHING YOU'RE NOT.
NEVER LET ANYONE DO THAT TO YOU.
NO MATTER WHAT HAPPENS, YOU BELONG TO *NO ONE.* YOU WILL BE CONTROLLED BY *NO ONE.* SWEAR IT TO ME, MAIKA.
I WILL KILL ANYONE WHO TELLS YOU OTHERWISE.
YOU CONTROL ME, THOUGH. I'M *YOURS.*
I GAVE UP THAT DREAM A LONG TIME AGO.
YOU HAVE A LIFE TO CONQUER. AN ENTIRE *WORLD* YOU MUST WAKE.
I HAVE SEEN IT. IT IS ALREADY SO.
WHAT THAT WORLD BECOMES... WILL DEPEND ENTIRELY ON THE STRENGTH OF YOUR HEART.

AND YOUR HEART, MY LITTLE WOLF, IS VERY STRONG.

ELSEWHERE.

FATHER, PERHAPS TOMORROW WE SHOULD...
...OH, GODDESS...
FATHER? WHAT HAPPENED?
YOU'RE BLEEDING.
IT IS THE MASK.
SHE MUST HAVE SOMEHOW FOUND THE STRENGTH TO PUT IT ON. HOW VERY STRANGE. I WAS NEVER ABLE TO SO MUCH AS TOUCH ANY OF THE FRAGMENTS.
GHOUL KILLER STRIKES AGA

FINISH YOUR MEAL, CHILD. WE MUST GO.
BUT... YOUR CHEST.
I WILL NOT TELL YOU AGAIN.
YES... *FATHER.*
CAN YOU NOT SENSE IT, CHILD?
THE BLOOD IS AWAKE.
OUR TIME... HAS COME AROUND... AT LAST.
TO BE CONTINUED...

Grim Haven
The Burned Coast
Dammarung
The Holy City of Aurum
Orleen
Pontus
Zamora
The Abyssal Sea
Thyria
The Known World

Arkangelus
ne
The Cloistened
Realm
(the Dusk Court)
The Dawn
Court
The Hidden Sea
Nanshi
Typhon
Kettara
The Fearing Sea
Salawan
The Dragon
Isles
e Cape of Bone
N
E
W
S

CREATORS

MARJORIE LIU is an attorney and *New York Times* bestselling author of over seventeen novels. Her comic book work includes *X-23, Black Widow, Dark Wolverine,* and *Astonishing X-Men,* for which she was nominated for a GLAAD Media Award for outstanding media images of the lesbian, gay, bisexual and transgender community. She teaches a course on comic book writing at MIT, and lives in Cambridge, MA.

SANA TAKEDA is an illustrator and comic book artist who was born in Niigata, and now resides in Tokyo, Japan. At age 20 she started out as a 3D CGI designer for SEGA, a Japanese video game company, and became a freelance artist when she was 25. She is still an artist, and has worked on titles such as *X-23* and *Ms. Marvel* for Marvel Comics, and is an illustrator for trading card games in Japan.

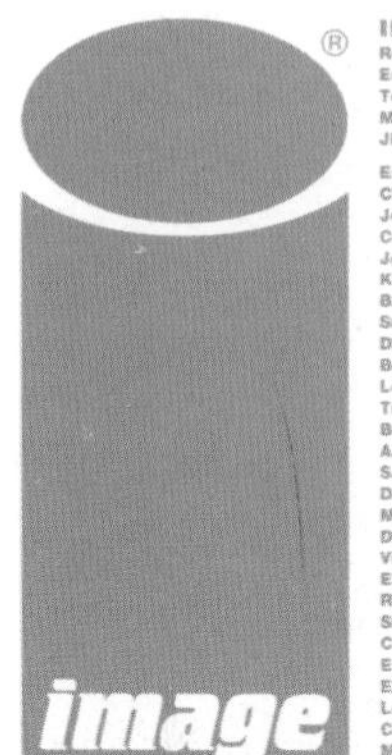

IMAGE COMICS, INC.

Robert Kirkman—Chief Operating Officer
Erik Larsen—Chief Financial Officer
Todd McFarlane—President
Marc Silvestri—Chief Executive Officer
Jim Valentino—Vice-President

Eric Stephenson—Publisher
Corey Murphy—Director of Sales
Jeff Boison—Director of Publishing Planning & Book Trade Sales
Chris Ross—Director of Digital Sales
Jeff Stang—Director of Specialty Sales
Kat Salazar—Director of PR & Marketing
Branwyn Bigglestone—Controller
Sue Korpela—Accounts Manager
Drew Gill—Art Director
Brett Warnock—Production Manager
Leigh Thomas—Print Manager
Tricia Ramos—Traffic Manager
Briah Skelly—Publicist
Aly Hoffman—Events & Conventions Coordinator
Sasha Head—Sales & Marketing Production Designer
David Brothers—Branding Manager
Melissa Gifford—Content Manager
Drew Fitzgerald—Publicity Assistant
Vincent Kukua—Production Artist
Erika Schnatz—Production Artist
Ryan Brewer—Production Artist
Shanna Matuszak—Production Artist
Carey Hall—Production Artist
Esther Kim—Direct Market Sales Representative
Emilio Bautista—Digital Sales Representative
Leanna Caunter—Accounting Assistant
Chloe Ramos-Peterson—Library Market Sales Representative
Maria Eizik—Administrative Assistant
IMAGECOMICS.COM

MONSTRESS™ Volume 2. First printing. July 2017. Published by Image Comics, Inc. Office of publication: 2701 NW Vaughn St., Suite 780, Portland, OR 97210.

Copyright © 2017 Marjorie Liu & Sana Takeda. All rights reserved. Originally published in single magazine form as MONSTRESS #7-12. MONSTRESS™ (including all prominent characters featured herein), its logo and all character likenesses are trademarks of Marjorie Liu & Sana Takeda, unless otherwise noted. "Image" and the Image Comics logos are registered trademarks of Image Comics, Inc. No part of this publication may be reproduced or transmitted, in any form or by any means (except for short excerpts for review purposes) without the express written permission of Image Comics, Inc. All names, characters, events and locales in this publication are entirely fictional. Any resemblance to actual persons (living or dead), events or places, without satiric intent, is coincidental. Printed in the USA. For information regarding the CPSIA on this printed material call: 203-595-3636 and provide reference # RICH – 736491. For international rights inquiries, contact: foreignlicensing@imagecomics.com.

Standard Cover ISBN: 978-1-5343-0041-5
Barnes & Noble Variant ISBN: 978-1-5343-0388-1
Newbury Comics Variant ISBN: 978-1-5343-0417-8
Dragon's Lair Comics Variant ISBN: 978-1-5343-0418-5
Forbidden Planet Variant ISBN: 978-1-5343-0419-2
Convention Hardcover Variant ISBN: 978-1-5343-0455-0
Creator Exclusive Variant ISBN: 978-1-5343-0454-3